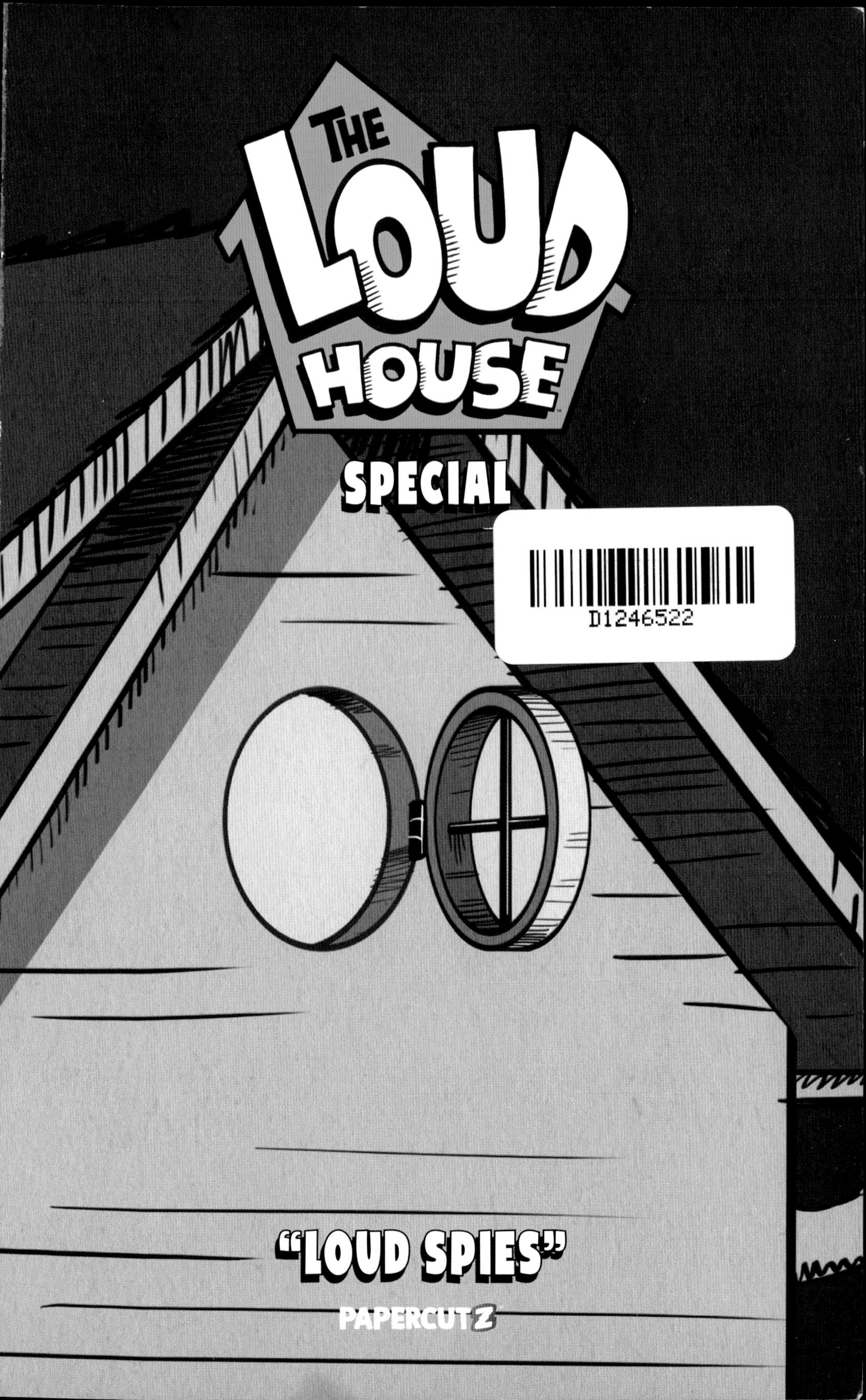
THE LOUD HOUSE
SPECIAL
"LOUD SPIES"
PAPERCUTZ

THE LOUD HOUSE

SPECIAL
"LOUD SPIES"

"CLUES AND BALLOONS"
Mikey Levitt — Writer
Erin Hyde — Artist, Colorist
Wilson Ramos Jr. — Letterer

"OPERATION B.U.T.T."
Kayla Parker — Writer
Amanda Lioi — Artist, Colorist
Wilson Ramos Jr. — Letterer

"DEEP COVER DOG"
Caitlin Fein — Writer
Izzy Boyce-Blanchard — Artist, Colorist
Wilson Ramos Jr. — Letterer

"STICKY FINGERS"
Jair Holguin — Writer
Olivia Walden — Artist, Colorist
Wilson Ramos Jr. — Letterer

"DEEP SEA LILY"
Jair Holguin — Writer
David Martin — Artist
Erin Rodriguez — Colorist
Wilson Ramos Jr. — Letterer

"COCKROACH APPROACH"
Paloma Uribe — Writer
Lex Hobson — Artist, Colorist
Wilson Ramos Jr. — Letterer

"ALICE FORGIVEN"
Derek Fridolfs — Writer
Izzy Boyce-Blanchard — Artist
Erin Rodriguez — Colorist
Wilson Ramos Jr. — Letterer

"THE NAME'S CHARLES. DOG CHARLES."
Kiernan Sjursen-Lien — Writer
Daniela De La Peña Rodriguez — Artist
Zazo Aguiar — Colorist
Wilson Ramos Jr. — Letterer

"FRIENDSHIP BRACESWEATS"
Kiernan Sjursen-Lien — Writer
Amanda Lioi — Artist
Erin Rodriguez — Colorist
Wilson Ramos Jr. — Letterer

"BUBBLE TROUBLE"
Erik Steinman — Writer
Lex Hobson — Artist, Colorist
Wilson Ramos Jr. — Letterer

"SNEAK PEEK"
Paloma Uribe — Writer
Alexia Valentine — Artist
Erin Rodriguez — Colorist
Wilson Ramos Jr. — Letterer

"DAVID STEELE SPECIAL FEATURE"
Andrew Brooks — Writer
Mad Cave Design Team — Design

"THE CASAGRANDES #6 PREVIEW"
Erik Steinman — Writer
Jennifer Hernandez — Artist, Colorist
Wilson Ramos Jr. — Letterer

LEX HOBSON — Cover Artist

JAYJAY JACKSON — Design

NEIL WADE, GABRIELLE DOLBEY, DANA CLUVERIUS, MOLLIE FREILICH, and ARTHUR "DJ" DESIN — Special Thanks

STEPHANIE BROOKS — Editor

JEFF WHITMAN — Comics Editor/Nickelodeon

MICOL HIATT — Comics Designer/Nickelodeon

MIKE MARTS — Editor in Chief

LAURA CHACÓN - Founder • MARK LONDON - CEO and Chief Creative Officer • MARK IRWIN - Senior Vice President • MIKE MARTS - EVP and Editor-in-Chief
CHRIS FERNANDEZ – Publisher • ZOHRA ASHPARI – Senior Editor • STEPHANIE BROOKS – Editor • GIOVANNA T. OROZCO – Production Manager
MIGUEL A. ZAPATA - Design Director • DIANA BERMÚDEZ - Graphic Designer • DAVID REYES - Graphic Designer • SEBASTIAN RAMIREZ - Graphic Designer
ADRIANA T. OROZCO - Interactive Media Designer • NICOLÁS ZEA ARIAS - Audiovisual Production • CECILIA MEDINA - Chief Financial Officer
STARLIN GONZALEZ - Accounting Director • KURT NELSON - Director of Sales • ALLISON POND - Marketing Director • MAYA LOPEZ - Marketing Manager
JAMES FACCINTO - Publicist • GEOFFREY LAPID - Sales & Marketing Specialist • SPENSER NELLIS - Marketing Coordinator
CHRIS LA TORRE - Retail Relations Manager • CHRISTINA HARRINGTON - Direct Market Sales Coordinator • PEDRO HERRERA - Retail Associate
FRANK SILVA - Executive Assistant • STEPHANIE HIDALGO - Office Manager

Papercutz was founded by Terry Nantier and Jim Salicrup.

ISBN: 978-1-5458-1063-7 paperback edition
ISBN: 978-1-5458-1062-0 hardcover edition

Printed in China
November 2023

First Printing

MEET THE L[redacted] F[redacted]MIL[redacted]

and friends!

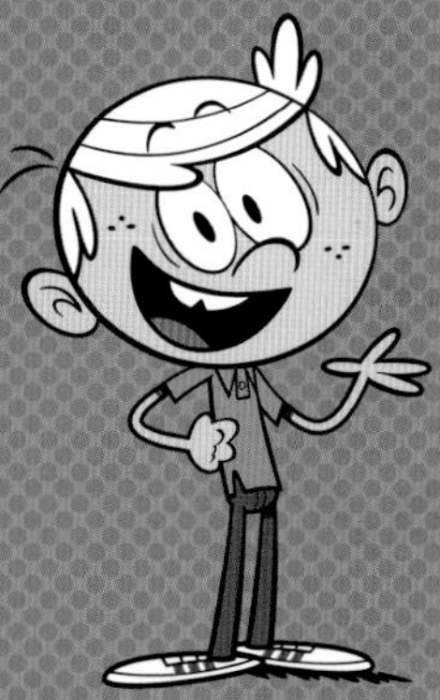

LINCOLN LOUD
THE MIDDLE CHILD

Lincoln is the middle child, with five older sisters and five younger sisters. He has learned that surviving the Loud household means staying a step ahead. As the "man with a plan," he's always coming up with a way to get what he wants or deal with a problem, even if things inevitably go wrong. But don't worry, Lincoln's got a backup plan for that, too. He loves comicbooks, video games, magic, fantasy and science fiction stories – all of which you might find him enjoying in his underwear. His favorite characters include secret agent David Steele (think James Bond), superhero Ace Savvy (think Superman with a knack for playing-card puns) and video game protagonist Muscle Fish.
He and his best friend Clyde make up the dynamic duo, Clincoln McCloud! They, along with his best friends (collectively known as "the Action News Team" because of the reporting they do for the school news program), always stick together – it's the best way to survive middle school.

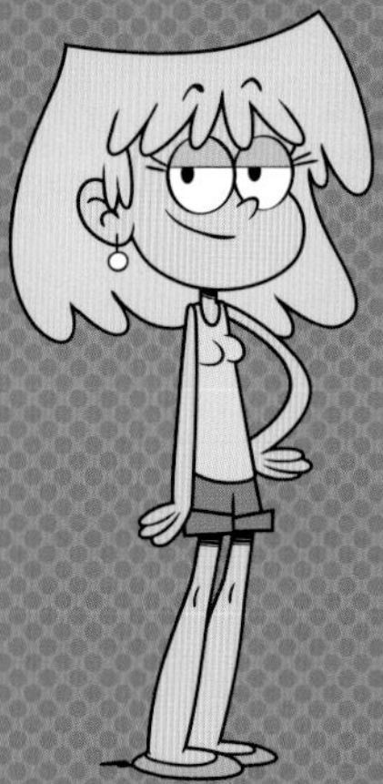

LORI LOUD
THE OLDEST

Lori's the first-born child of the Loud clan, and therefore sees herself as the boss of all her siblings. She feels she's paved the way for them and deserves extra respect. Her signature traits are rolling her eyes, texting her boyfriend Bobby (AKA "Boo-Boo Bear"), and literally saying "literally" all the time. Because she's the oldest and most experienced sibling, Lori can be a great ally, so it pays to stay on her good side, especially since she can drive.
Lori has begun attending Fairway University, a prestigious golf college, and is one of the youngest players to make the school's golf team. Even though she's moved away from home, she's always in touch with her siblings. Even at college, Lori is always part of the Loud family shenanigans.

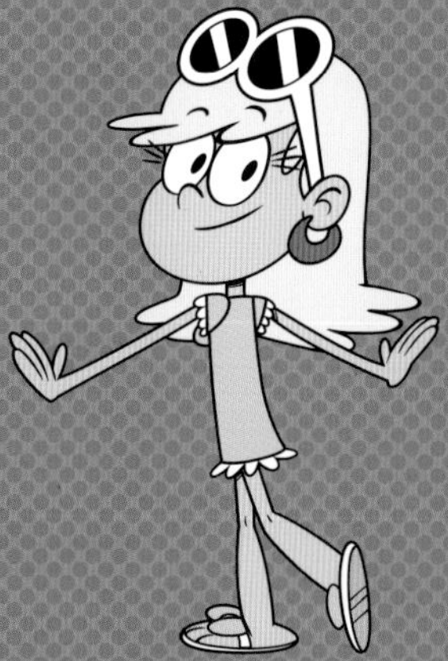

LENI LOUD
THE FASHIONISTA

Leni spends most of her time designing outfits, accessorizing, and shopping at the mall – which makes her the perfect sales employee at Reininger's department store. Her people-pleasing nature, natural leadership abilities, and fashion instincts keep customers coming back! Leni is supported by her best friends and co-workers, Miguel and Fiona (and sometimes Tanya the mannequin). And now she has the added support of her new boyfriend, Gavin, who works in the mall food court.
Back at the house, she always falls for Luan's pranks, and sometimes walks into walls when she's talking (she's not great at doing two things at once). But what Leni lacks in smarts, she makes up for in heart. She's the sweetest Loud around!

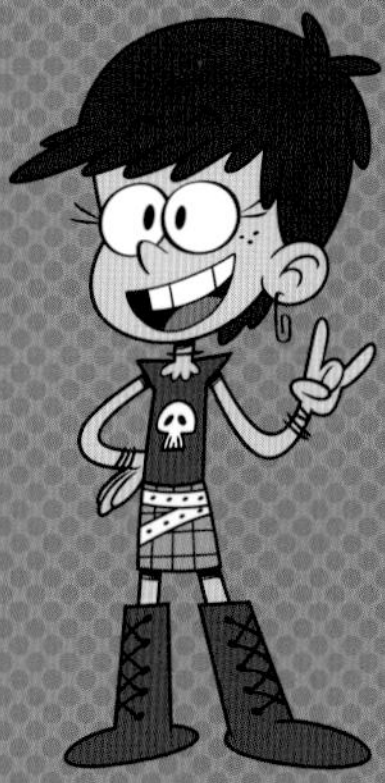

LUNA LOUD
THE ROCK STAR

Luna is loud, boisterous and freewheeling, and her energy is always cranked to 11. On the off-chance she doesn't have her guitar with her, everything can and will be turned into a musical instrument. You can always count on Luna to help out, and she'll do most anything you ask, as long as you're okay with her supplying a rocking musical accompaniment.
When she's not jamming, Luna is most likely hanging out with her girlfriend, Sam, or playing with their band, The Moon Goats. The two might even be found babysitting the McBride's cats – it turns out Sam's a natural cat whisperer!

MR COCONUTS

Luan Loud's wisecracking dummy.

LUAN LOUD
THE JOKESTER

Luan is a standup comedienne who provides a nonstop barrage of silly puns. She's big on prop comedy – squirting flowers and whoopee cushions – so you have to be on your toes whenever she's around. She loves to pull pranks – April Fool's Day is her favorite day (and the rest of the Louds' least favorite). Luan is also a really good ventriloquist – she is often found doing bits with her dummy, Mr. Coconuts (but don't let him hear you calling him a "dummy"). At school, Luan and her boyfriend, Benny, are usually writing and performing in the high school's theatrical productions – under the somewhat melodramatic supervision of their drama teacher, Mrs. Bernardo. Luan has also reached new heights while playing Dairyland character Heidi Heifer during the theme park's season.

LYNN LOUD
THE ATHLETE

Lynn is athletic, full of energy, and always looking for a challenge or competition. She can turn anything into a sport. Putting away eggs? Jump shot! Score! Cleaning up the eggs? Slap shot! Score! Despite her competitive nature, Lynn always tries to have a good time with her family... and her teammates and best friends Paula and Margo. At school, she takes her duties as hall monitor seriously and doesn't tolerate any slackers... but she also shows a lot of heart when looking after Lincoln in his first year at middle school. One super fun fact about Lynn: her name is really Lynn Jr. (L.J.), because she's named after Dad!

LUCY LOUD
THE EMO

Lucy can always be counted on to give the morbid point of view in any given situation. She is obsessed with all things spooky and dark – funerals, vampires, séances... you get the idea. Lucy has a way of mysteriously appearing out of nowhere, and try as they might, her siblings never get used to this. She loves the character of Edwin from the TV show "Vampires of Melancholia," and has a homemade bust of him hidden in her closet.

Lucy spends most of her time with her friends in the Morticians Club, of which she's a co-president. Together, the club speaks to spirits, attends casket conventions, and rides around in a hearse (well, technically it's just a station wagon painted black). Their motto is "Keep Calm and Embalm."

LOLA LOUD
THE BEAUTY QUEEN

Lola is a pageant powerhouse whose interests include glitter, photo shoots, and her own beautiful, beautiful face. But don't let her cute, gap-toothed smile fool you; underneath all the sugar and spice lurks a Machiavellian mastermind. Whatever Lola wants, Lola gets – or else. She's the eyes and ears of the household and never resists an opportunity to tattle on troublemakers. But if you stay on Lola's good side, you've got yourself a fierce ally – and a credit line to the first national bank of Lola. She might even let you drive her around in her pink jeep while she practices her pageant wave.

LANA LOUD
THE TOMBOY

Lana is the rough-and-tumble sparkplug counterpart to her twin sister, Lola. She's all about animals, mud pies, and muffler repairs. She's the resident Ms. Fix-it and animal whisperer, and is always ready to lend a hand – the dirtier the job, the better. Need your toilet unclogged? Snake trained? Back-zit popped? Lana's your gal. All she asks in return is a handful of kibble (she often sneaks it from the dog bowl anyway) or anything you can fish out of a nearby garbage can. She's proud of who she is, and her big heart definitely overpowers her pungent dumpster smell. Needless to say, while the twins love each other deep down, they've been known to get into some pretty epic brawls, mud and sequins flying. But when they join forces (like the time they pretended to be each other for their own personal gain), the rest of the Louds had better look out.

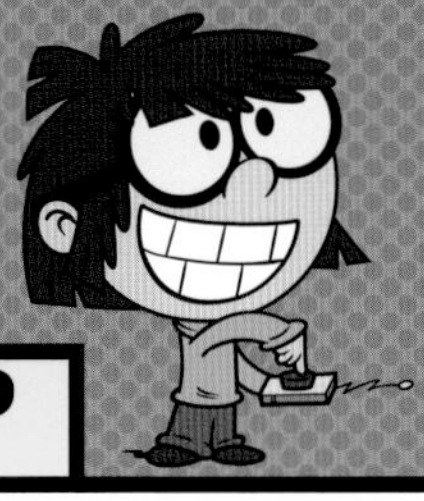

LISA LOUD
THE GENIUS

Lisa is smarter than the rest of her siblings combined, which would still be big news even if she wasn't only four years old. Lisa spends most of her time working in her bedroom lab (the family has gotten used to the explosions), and says her research leaves little time for frivolous pursuits like "playing" or "human interaction." Despite this, she can still find time to unwind with a little bit of West Coast rap. She has a collection of robot companions that she's created over the years, but these days relies mostly on Todd, her newest (and sassiest) mechanical friend. Together they've traveled back in time, launched themselves into outer space, and enjoyed many hours watching Todd's favorite TV show, "Robot Dance Party." At school (where Lisa is smarter than her teacher), she is learning to enjoy social interaction with her friend Darcy, but will forego nap time to work on all the top secret projects she's got going on with the Norwegian government.

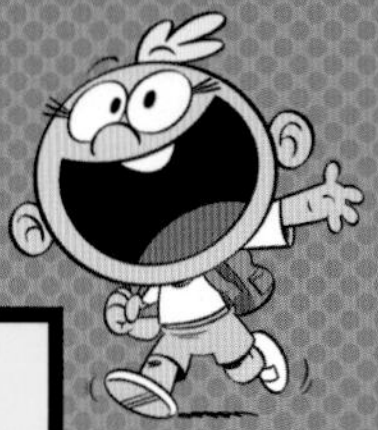

LILY LOUD
THE BABY

Lily's the baby of the family, but she's growing up fast. She's a toddler now and can speak full sentences– well, sometimes. As an infant she was already mischievous, but now she's upped her game. Her most important goal – other than tricking the family into taking her for ice cream – is to impress the other preschool kids at show and tell. No matter what, though, she still brings a smile to everyone's faces, and the family loves her unconditionally.

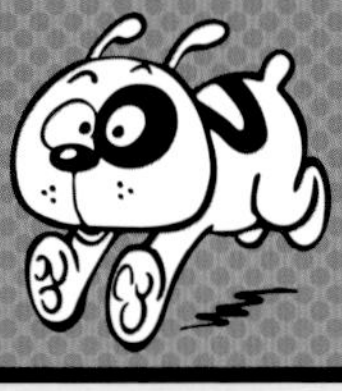

CHARLES

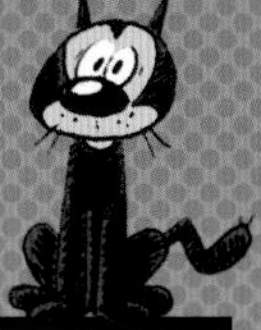

CLIFF

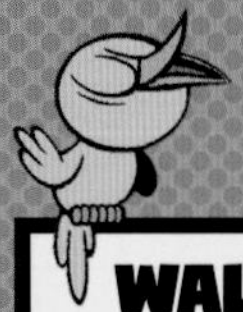

WALT

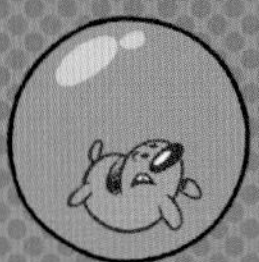

GEO

RITA LOUD

Mother to the eleven Loud kids, Mom Rita wears many different hats. She's a chauffeur, homework-checker and barf cleaner-upper all rolled into one. Mom is organized and keeps the family running like a well-oiled machine. She's always there for her kids and ready to jump into action during a crisis, whether it's a fight between the twins or finding Leni's missing shoe. When she's not chasing the kids, she's a columnist for the Royal Woods Gazette. As a skilled writer, she's able to connect with her readers as a mom simply trying to do her best. She also loves taking on house projects and is very handy with tools (guess that's where Lana gets it from). Between writing her novel, working on her column, and being a mom, her days are always hectic - but she wouldn't have it any other way.

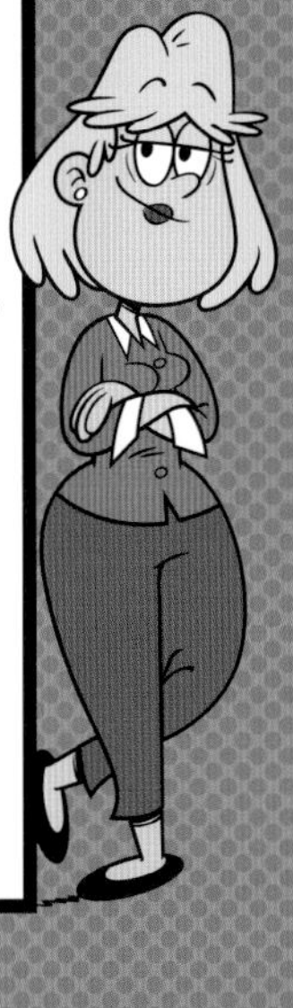

LYNN LOUD SR.

Dad (Lynn Loud Sr.) is a fun-loving, upbeat chef and owner of Lynn's Table – a family style restaurant that specializes in serving delicious but outrageously named meals like Lynn-sagna and Lynn-ger chicken. A sentimental kid-at-heart, he's not above taking part in the kids' zany schemes but is more well known for the emotions he wears on his sleeves: his sobbing – both for joy and sadness – is legendary. In addition to cooking, Dad loves his van (affectionately named Vanzilla), British culture, and making puns with any of the kids not already rolling their eyes. Most of all, Dad loves rocking out with his best friend and head waiter, Kotaro. They're part of a cowbell-focused band with some other dads in Royal Woods; hence their band name: The Doo-Dads.

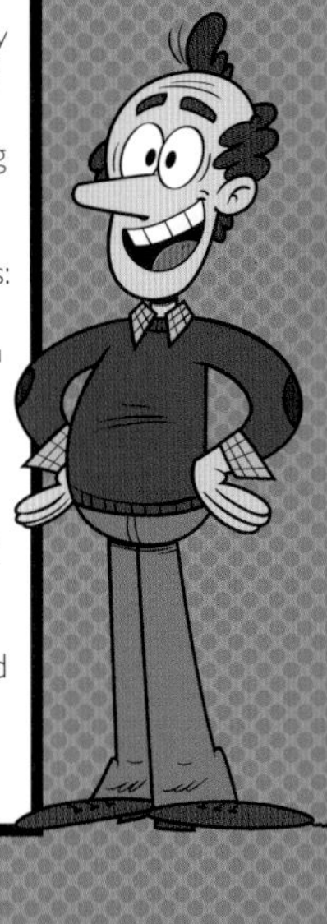

CLYDE McBRIDE

Clyde is Lincoln's best friend in the whole world… so it probably goes without saying that he's also Lincoln's partner in crime. Clyde is always willing to go along with Lincoln's crazy schemes, even if he sees the flaws in them up-front or if they sometimes give him anxiety tummy aches. Lincoln and Clyde are two peas in a pod and share pretty much all of the same tastes in movies, comics, TV shows, toys—you name it. Clyde knows exactly who he is and is not afraid to show it! As an only child, Clyde envies Lincoln—how cool would it be to always have siblings around to talk to? But since Clyde spends so much time at the Loud house, he's almost an honorary sibling anyway. Clyde is a little neurotic, but that's probably because he's the son of helicopter dads, Howard and Harold. They are VERY over-protective and VERY involved in his life. Clyde isn't spoiled, he's just extremely well-cared for. But he's slowly learning to stand on his own two feet and his dads are starting to see how well he can take care of himself.

ZACH GURDLE

Lincoln's pal Zach is a self-admitted nerd who's obsessed with aliens and conspiracy theories. (He's just following in the footsteps of his alien hunting parents.) Zach lives between a freeway and a circus, so the chaos of the Loud House doesn't faze him. To Zach, everything is a mystery to be solved or coverup to be exposed. His best friend in the gang is Rusty, with whom he occasionally butts heads. But deep down, it's all love.

RUSTY SPOKES

Lincoln's friend Rusty is a self-proclaimed ladies' man who's always the first to dish out girl advice— even though he's never been on an actual date. No one has more confidence than Rusty, even if that confidence is often completely misguided. Rusty's a looker – at least in his own eyes – and is always working hard to protect his face (what he calls his "moneymaker"). Rusty is always sharing advice from his experienced but equally delusional cousin, Derek. No matter what the situation, it seems like Derek's been there before and lived to tell about it. Rusty's dad, Rodney, owns a clothing store called "Duds for Dudes," so he can always hook the gang up with some dapper duds—just as long as no one gets anything dirty.

LIAM HUNNICUTT

Lincoln's friend Liam is an enthusiastic, sweet-natured farm boy full of down-home wisdom. He loves hanging out with his Mee Maw, wrestling his prize pig Virginia, and sharing his farm-to-table produce with the rest of the gang. No matter the situation, Liam faces it with optimism.

STELLA ZHAU

Lincoln's pal Stella is a tech genius, always building new devices – usually from parts she's salvaged from old devices. She loves to take things apart just to see how they work. Her smarts help keep the gang focused and on track, especially when they're chasing a news story. Stella will happily take charge of a situation – she's helped solve many a school mystery and even improved the gang's shield formation defense in dodgeball.

RONNIE ANNE SANTIAGO

Ronnie Anne's a skateboarding city girl now. She's fearless, free-spirited, and always quick to come up with a plan. She's one tough cookie, but she also has a sweet side. Ronnie Anne loves helping her family, and that's taught her to help others too. When she's not pitching in at the family *mercado*, you can find her exploring the neighborhood with her best friend Sid, or ordering hot dogs with her skater buds Casey, Nikki, and Sameer. Having a family as big as the Casagrandes has taught Ronnie Anne to deal with anything life throws her way.

BOBBY SANTIAGO

Bobby is Ronnie Anne's big bro. He's a student and one of the hardest workers in the city. He loves his family and loves working at the *mercado*. As his *abuelo's* right hand man, Bobby can't wait to take over the family business one day. He's a big kid at heart, and his clumsiness gets him into some sticky situations at work, like locking himself in the freezer. *Mercado* mishaps aside, everyone in the neighborhood loves to come to the store and talk to Bobby.

MARIA CASAGRANDE SANTIAGO

Maria is Bobby and Ronnie Anne's mom. As a nurse at the city hospital, she's hardworking and even harder to gross out. For years, Maria, Bobby, and Ronnie Anne were used to only having each other… but now that they've moved in with their Casagrande relatives, they're embracing big family life. Maria is the voice of reason in the household and known for her always-on-the-go attitude. Her long work hours means she doesn't always get to spend time with Bobby and Ronnie Anne; but when she does, she makes that time count.

CARLOTA CASAGRANDE

Carlota is CJ, Carl, and Carlitos' older sister. A social media influencer, she's excited to be like a big sister to Ronnie Anne. She's a force to be reckoned with, and is always trying to share her distinctive vintage style tips with Ronnie Anne.

CJ (CARLOS JR.) CASAGRANDE

CJ is Carlota's younger brother and Carl and Carlitos' older brother. He was born with Down Syndrome. He lights up any room with his infectious smile and is always ready to play. He's obsessed with pirates and is BFFs with Bobby. He likes to wear a bowtie to any family occasion, and you can always catch him laughing or helping his *abuela*.

CARL CASAGRANDE

Carl is wise beyond his years. He's confident, outgoing, and puts a lot of time and effort into looking good. He likes to think of himself as a suave businessman and doesn't like to get caught playing with his action figures or wearing his footie PJs. Even though Bobby is nothing but nice to him, Carl sees his big cousin as his biggest rival.

"CLUES & BALLOONS"

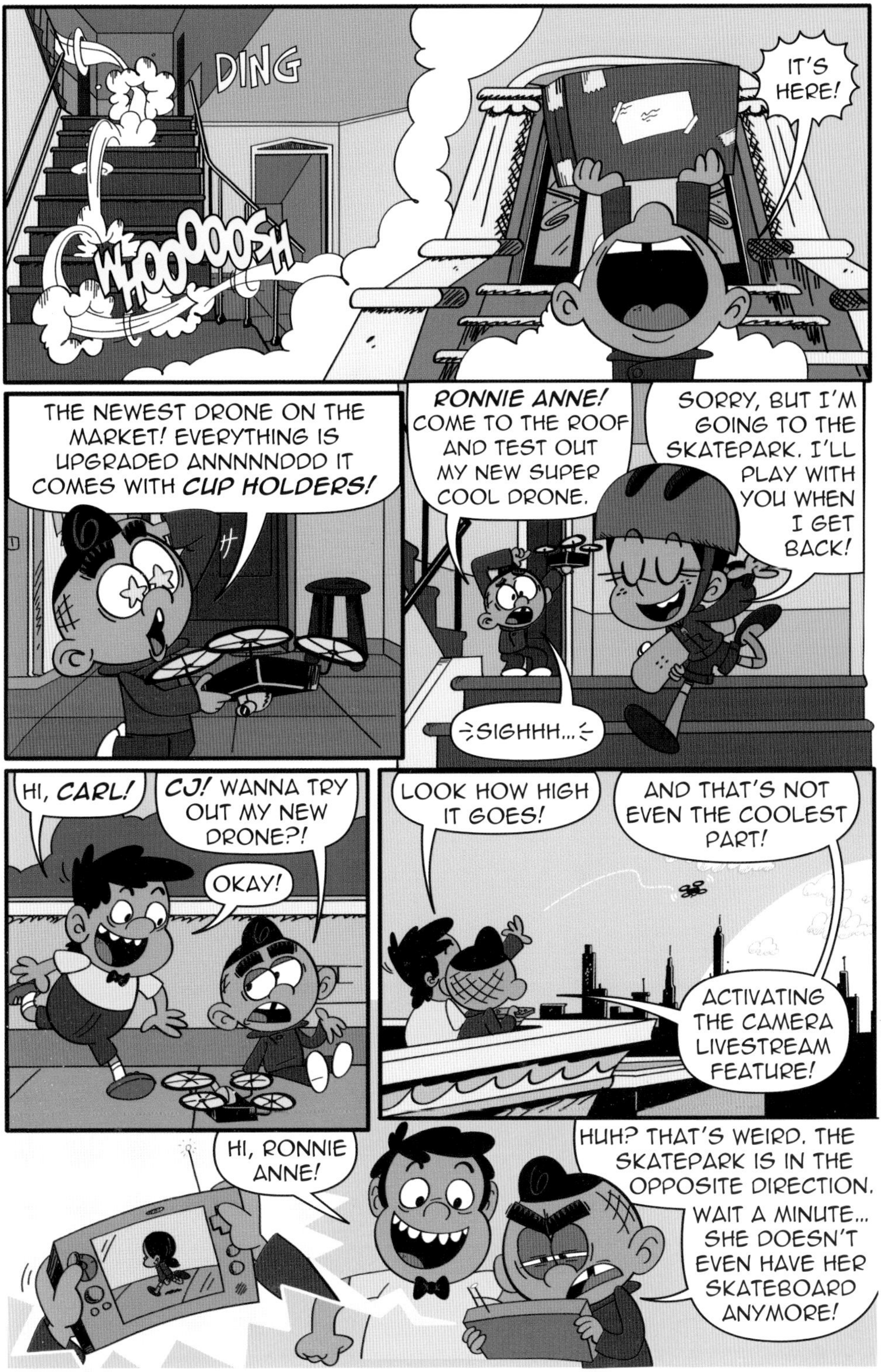

DING
WHOOOOOSH
IT'S HERE!
THE NEWEST DRONE ON THE MARKET! EVERYTHING IS UPGRADED ANNNNNDDD IT COMES WITH CUP HOLDERS!
RONNIE ANNE! COME TO THE ROOF AND TEST OUT MY NEW SUPER COOL DRONE.
SORRY, BUT I'M GOING TO THE SKATEPARK. I'LL PLAY WITH YOU WHEN I GET BACK!
SIGHHH...
HI, CARL!
CJ! WANNA TRY OUT MY NEW DRONE?!
OKAY!
LOOK HOW HIGH IT GOES!
AND THAT'S NOT EVEN THE COOLEST PART!
ACTIVATING THE CAMERA LIVESTREAM FEATURE!
HI, RONNIE ANNE!
HUH? THAT'S WEIRD. THE SKATEPARK IS IN THE OPPOSITE DIRECTION.
WAIT A MINUTE... SHE DOESN'T EVEN HAVE HER SKATEBOARD ANYMORE!

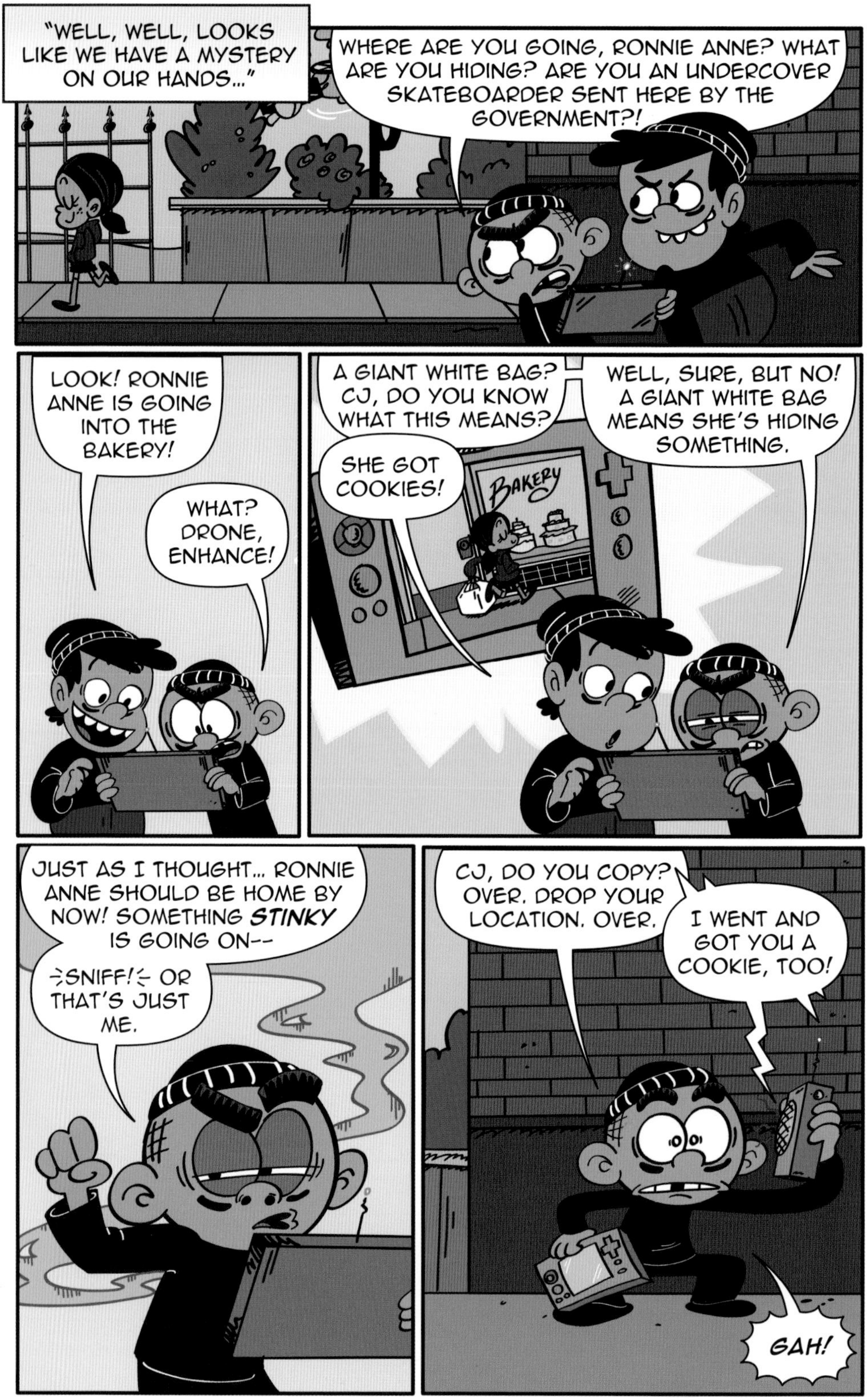
"WELL, WELL, LOOKS LIKE WE HAVE A MYSTERY ON OUR HANDS..."
WHERE ARE YOU GOING, RONNIE ANNE? WHAT ARE YOU HIDING? ARE YOU AN UNDERCOVER SKATEBOARDER SENT HERE BY THE GOVERNMENT?!
LOOK! RONNIE ANNE IS GOING INTO THE BAKERY!
WHAT? DRONE, ENHANCE!
A GIANT WHITE BAG? CJ, DO YOU KNOW WHAT THIS MEANS?
SHE GOT COOKIES!
BAKERY
WELL, SURE, BUT NO! A GIANT WHITE BAG MEANS SHE'S HIDING SOMETHING.
JUST AS I THOUGHT... RONNIE ANNE SHOULD BE HOME BY NOW! SOMETHING STINKY IS GOING ON--
SNIFF! OR THAT'S JUST ME.
CJ, DO YOU COPY? OVER. DROP YOUR LOCATION. OVER.
I WENT AND GOT YOU A COOKIE, TOO!
GAH!

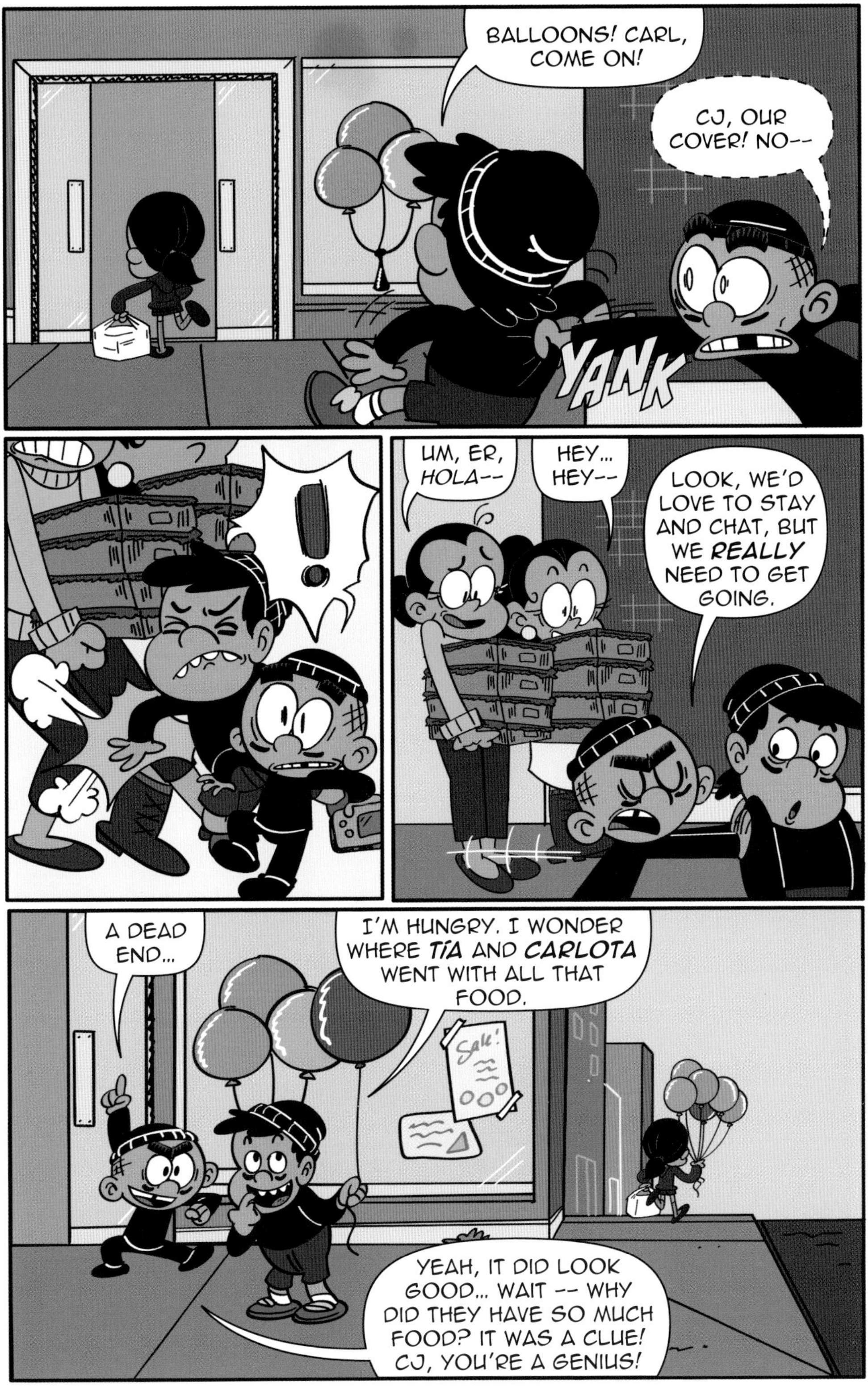
BALLOONS! CARL, COME ON!
CJ, OUR COVER! NO--
YANK
!
UM, ER, HOLA--
HEY... HEY--
LOOK, WE'D LOVE TO STAY AND CHAT, BUT WE REALLY NEED TO GET GOING.
A DEAD END...
I'M HUNGRY. I WONDER WHERE TÍA AND CARLOTA WENT WITH ALL THAT FOOD.
SALE!
YEAH, IT DID LOOK GOOD... WAIT -- WHY DID THEY HAVE SO MUCH FOOD? IT WAS A CLUE! CJ, YOU'RE A GENIUS!

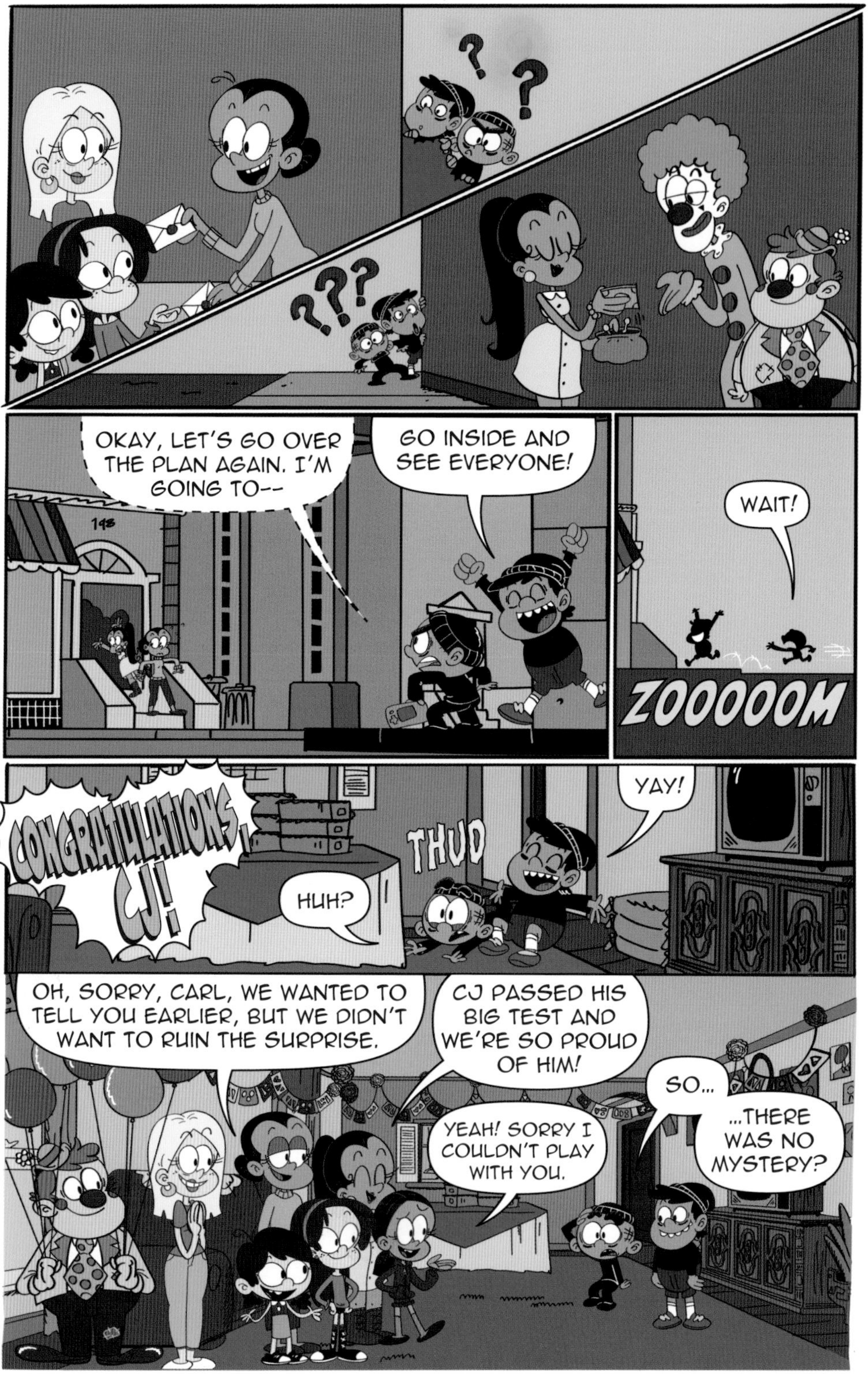
OKAY, LET'S GO OVER THE PLAN AGAIN. I'M GOING TO--
GO INSIDE AND SEE EVERYONE!
WAIT!
ZOOOOOM
CONGRATULATIONS, CJ!
THUD
YAY!
HUH?
OH, SORRY, CARL, WE WANTED TO TELL YOU EARLIER, BUT WE DIDN'T WANT TO RUIN THE SURPRISE.
CJ PASSED HIS BIG TEST AND WE'RE SO PROUD OF HIM!
YEAH! SORRY I COULDN'T PLAY WITH YOU.
SO...
...THERE WAS NO MYSTERY?

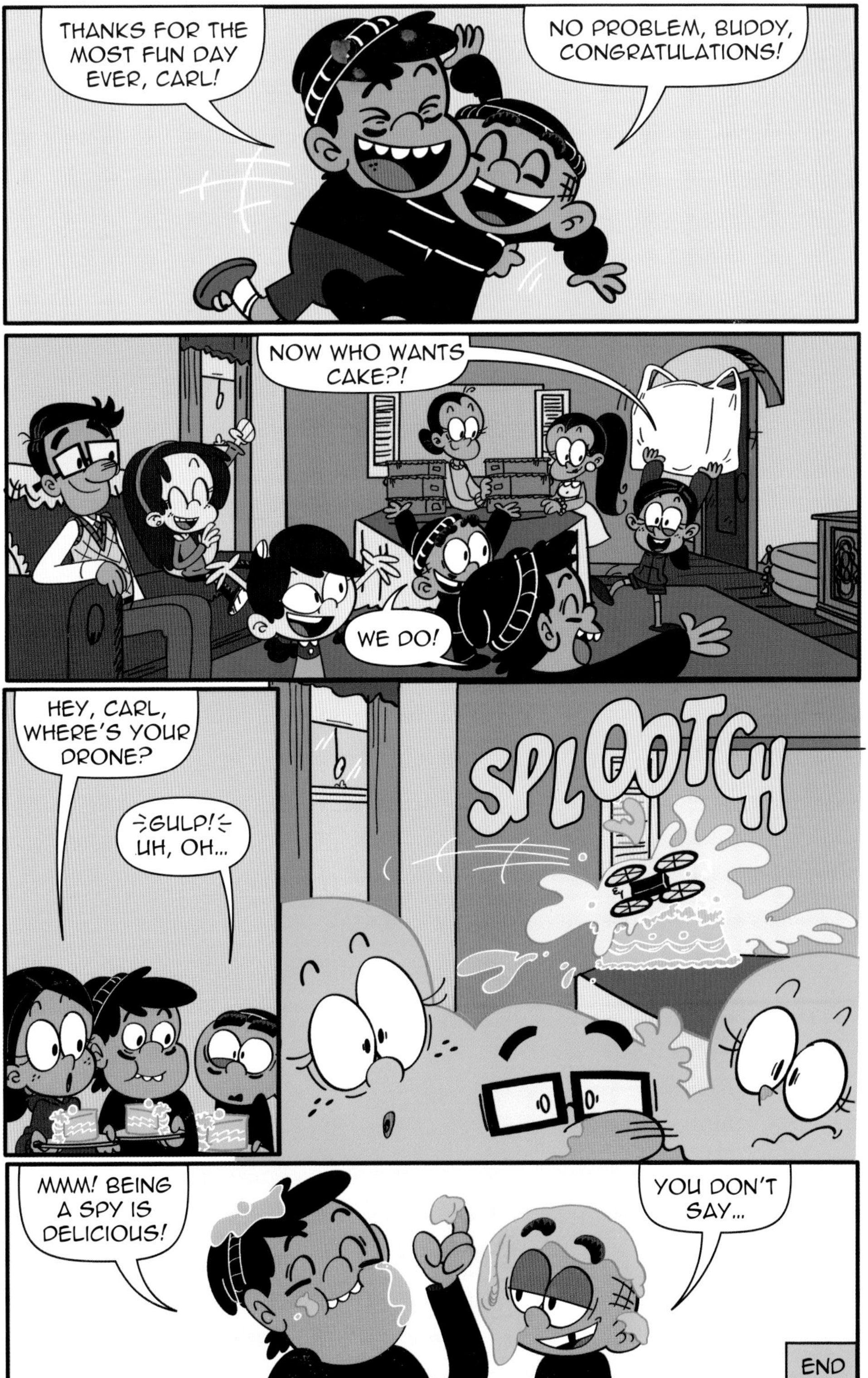
THANKS FOR THE MOST FUN DAY EVER, CARL!
NO PROBLEM, BUDDY, CONGRATULATIONS!
NOW WHO WANTS CAKE?!
WE DO!
HEY, CARL, WHERE'S YOUR DRONE?
GULP! UH, OH...
SPLOOTCH
MMM! BEING A SPY IS DELICIOUS!
YOU DON'T SAY...
END

"DEEP COVER DOG"

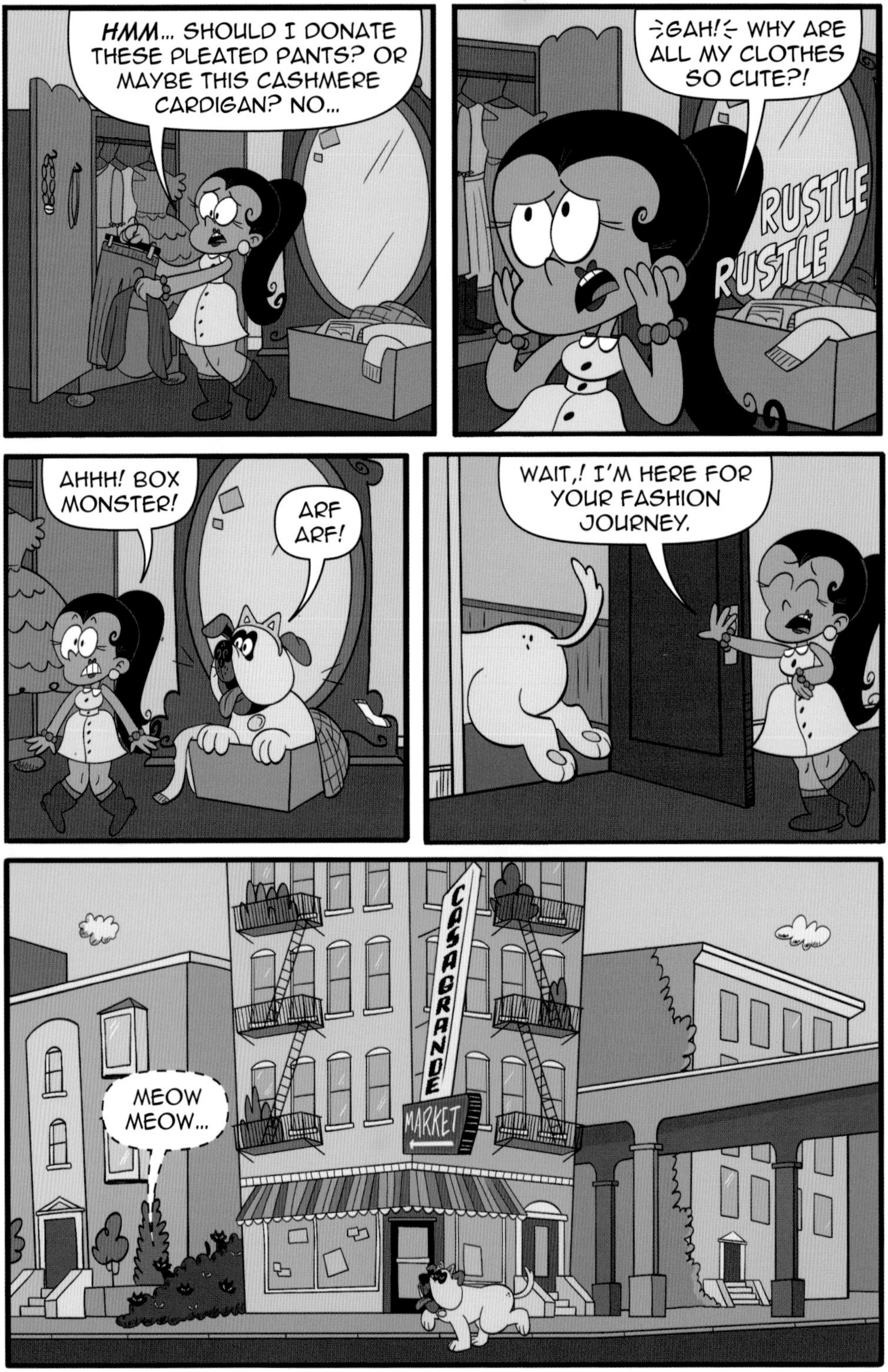

HMM... SHOULD I DONATE THESE PLEATED PANTS? OR MAYBE THIS CASHMERE CARDIGAN? NO...
GAH! WHY ARE ALL MY CLOTHES SO CUTE?!
RUSTLE
RUSTLE
AHHH! BOX MONSTER!
ARF ARF!
WAIT,! I'M HERE FOR YOUR FASHION JOURNEY.
CASAGRANDE
MARKET
MEOW MEOW...

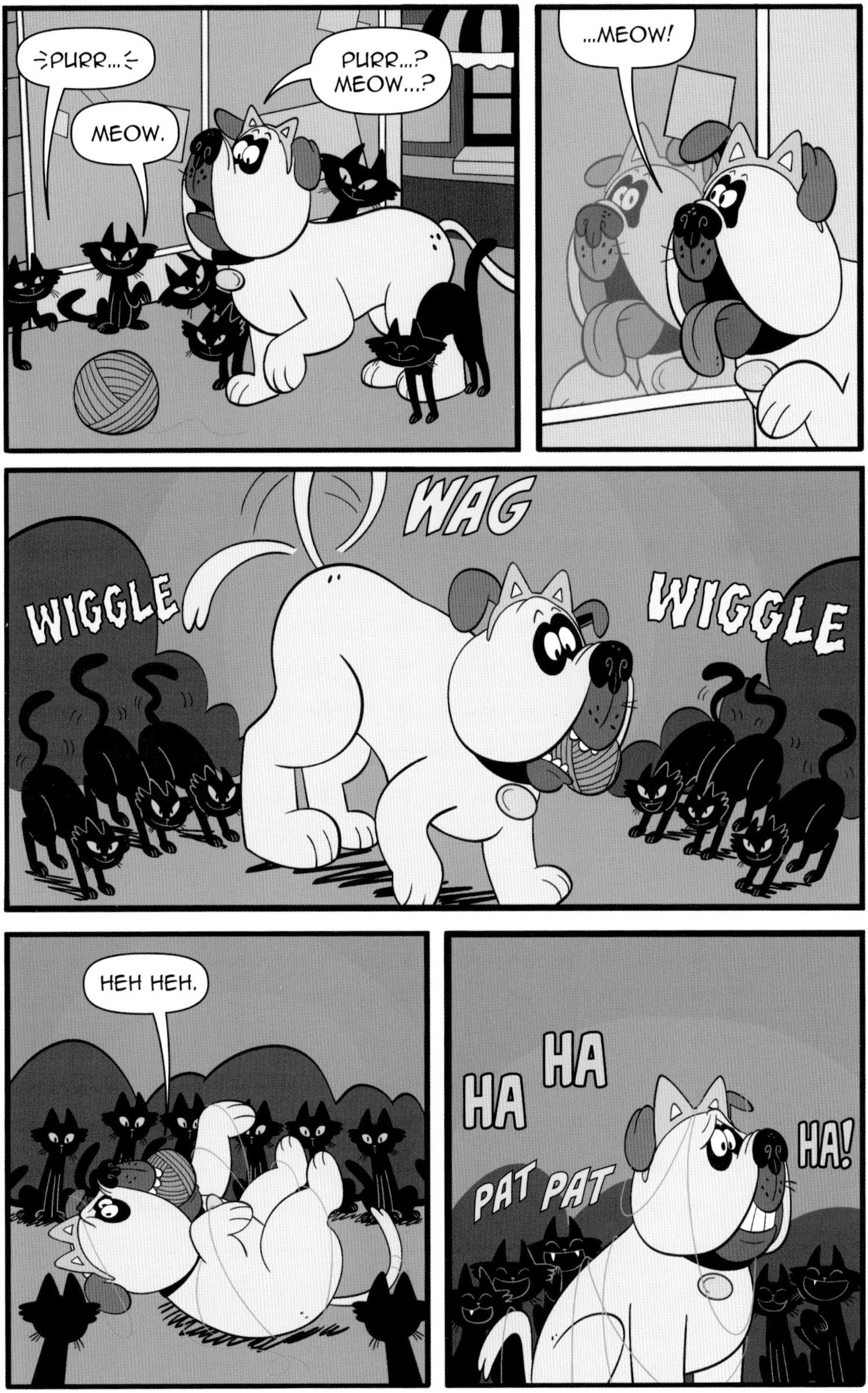
PURR...
MEOW.
PURR...? MEOW...?
...MEOW!
WAG
WIGGLE
WIGGLE
HEH HEH.
HA
HA
PAT PAT
HA!

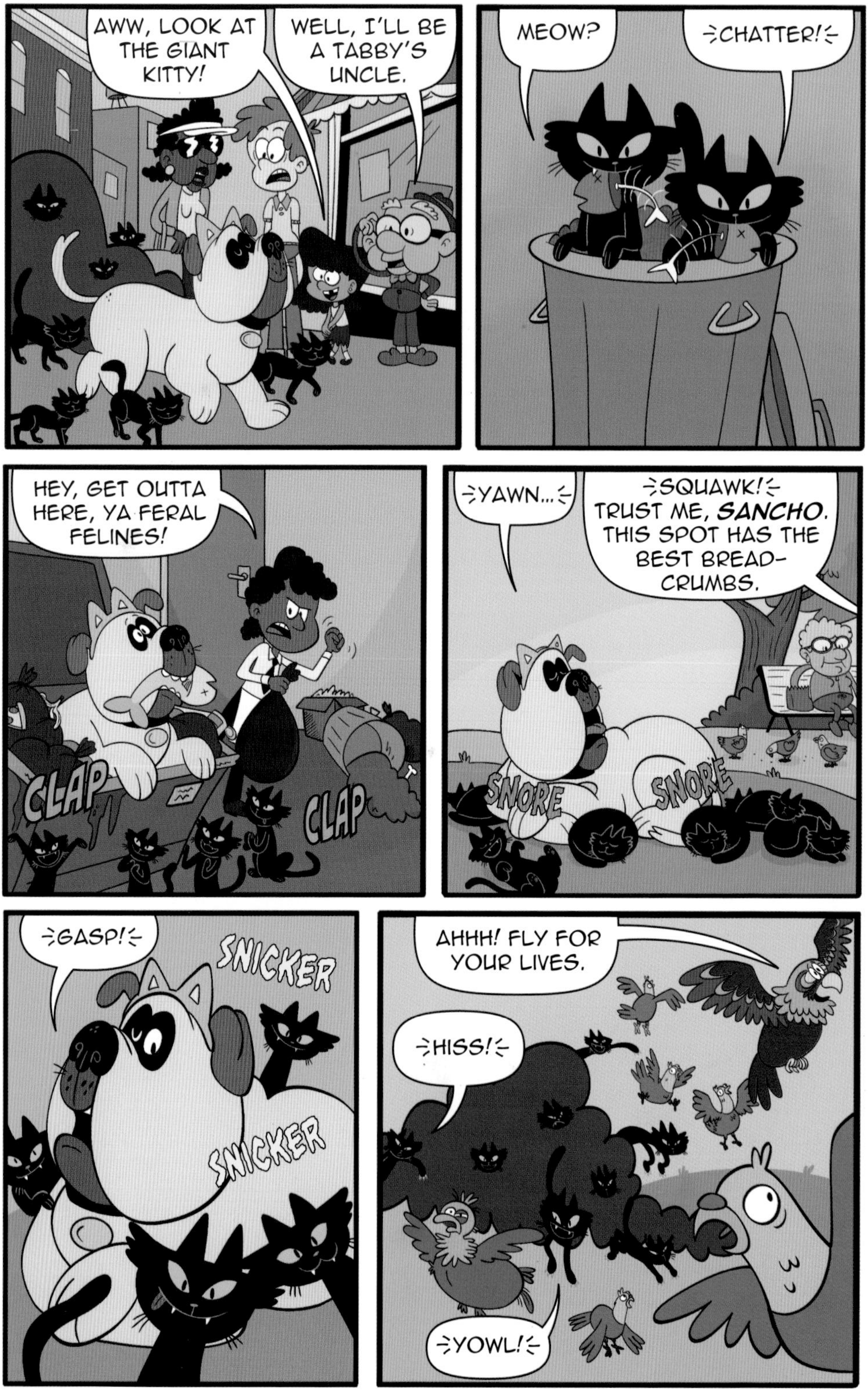
AWW, LOOK AT THE GIANT KITTY!
WELL, I'LL BE A TABBY'S UNCLE.
MEOW?
CHATTER!
HEY, GET OUTTA HERE, YA FERAL FELINES!
CLAP
CLAP
YAWN...
SQUAWK! TRUST ME, SANCHO. THIS SPOT HAS THE BEST BREAD-CRUMBS.
SNORE
SNORE
GASP!
SNICKER
SNICKER
AHHH! FLY FOR YOUR LIVES.
HISS!
YOWL!

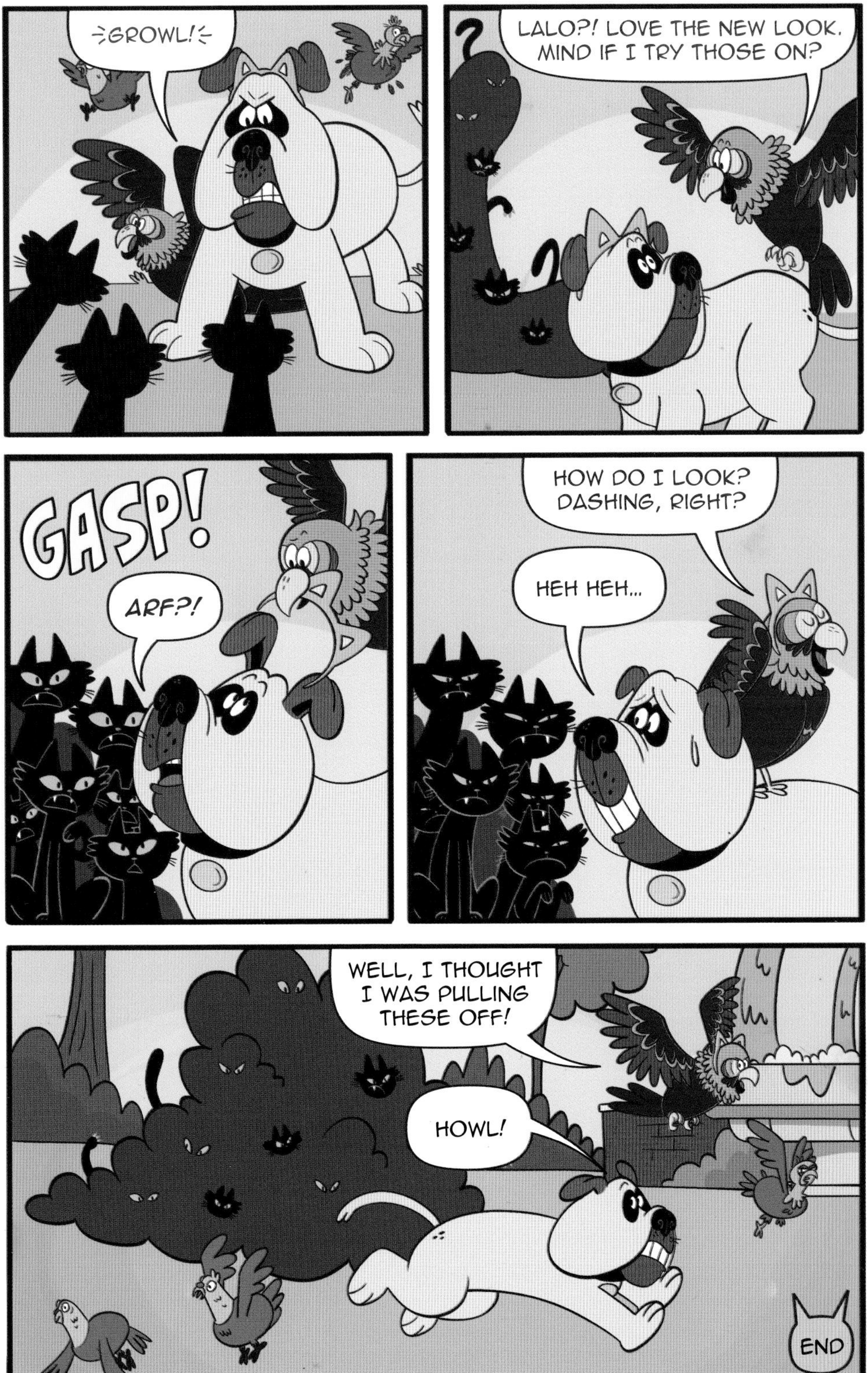
GROWL!
LALO?! LOVE THE NEW LOOK. MIND IF I TRY THOSE ON?
GASP!
ARF?!
HOW DO I LOOK? DASHING, RIGHT?
HEH HEH...
WELL, I THOUGHT I WAS PULLING THESE OFF!
HOWL!
END

"DEEP SEA LILY"

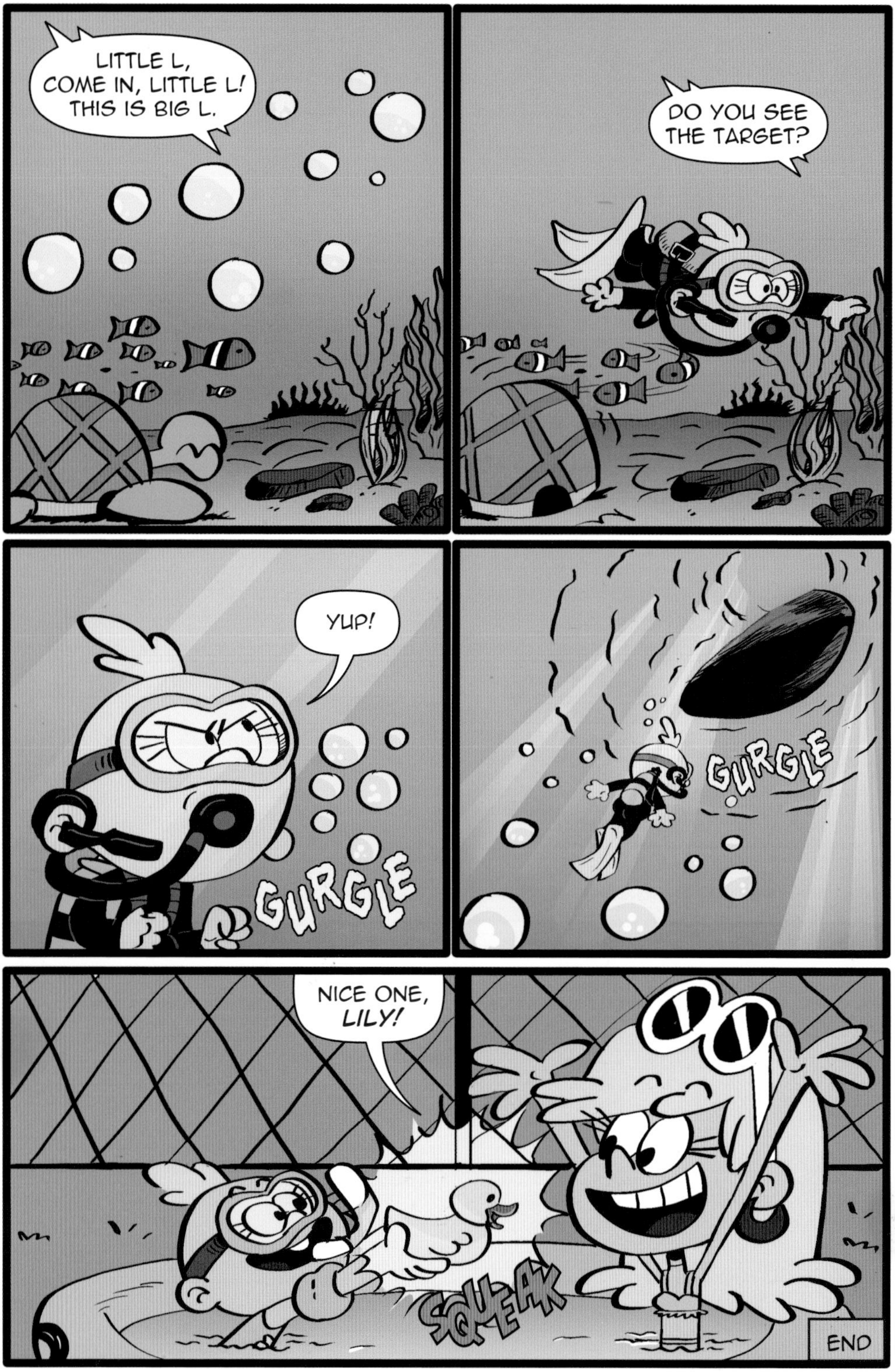

LITTLE L, COME IN, LITTLE L! THIS IS BIG L.
DO YOU SEE THE TARGET?
YUP!
GURGLE
GURGLE
NICE ONE, LILY!
SQUEAK
END

“ALI ORGI ”

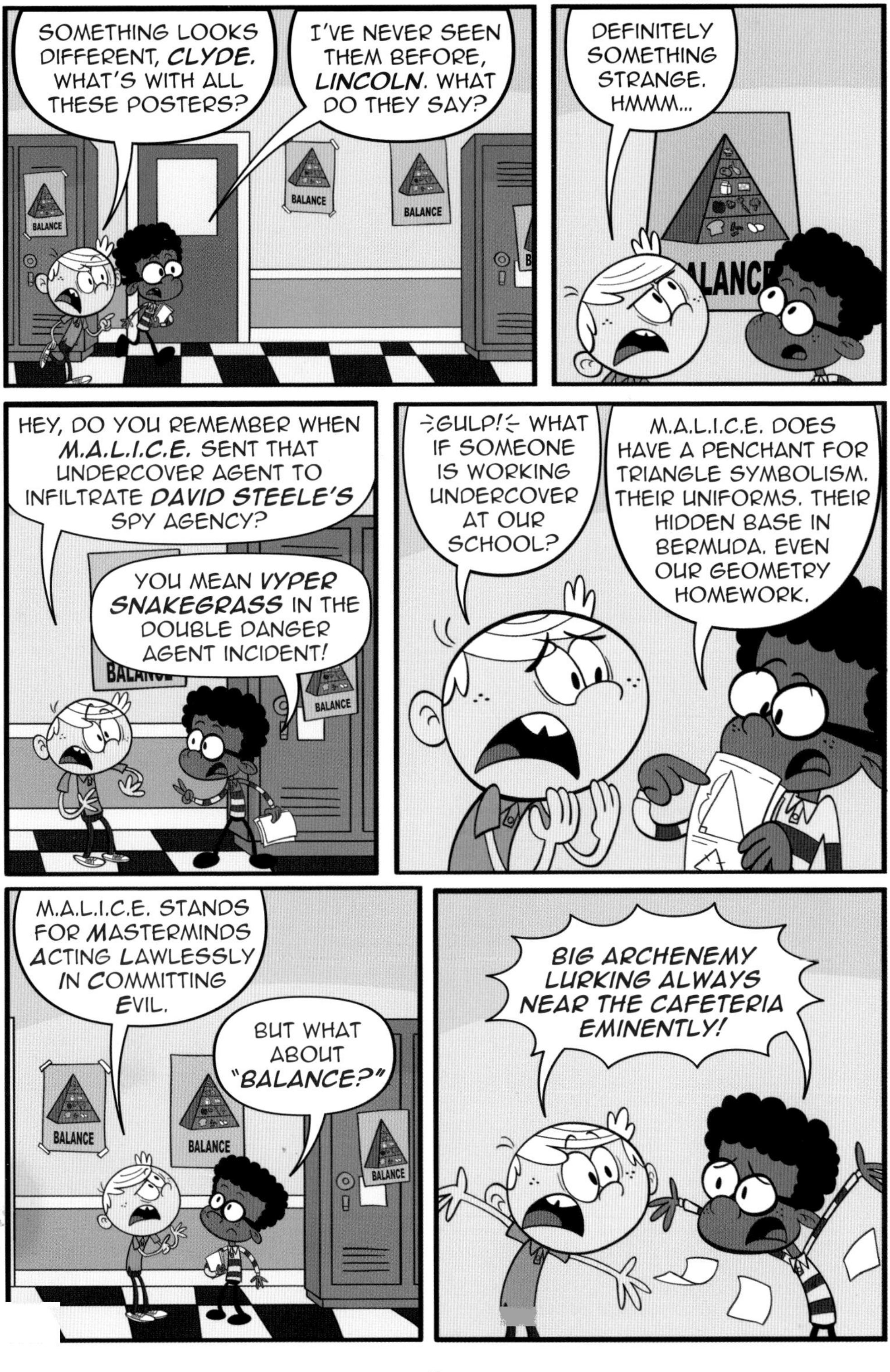

SOMETHING LOOKS DIFFERENT, CLYDE. WHAT'S WITH ALL THESE POSTERS?
I'VE NEVER SEEN THEM BEFORE, LINCOLN. WHAT DO THEY SAY?
BALANCE
DEFINITELY SOMETHING STRANGE. HMMM...
HEY, DO YOU REMEMBER WHEN M.A.L.I.C.E. SENT THAT UNDERCOVER AGENT TO INFILTRATE DAVID STEELE'S SPY AGENCY?
YOU MEAN VYPER SNAKEGRASS IN THE DOUBLE DANGER AGENT INCIDENT!
GULP! WHAT IF SOMEONE IS WORKING UNDERCOVER AT OUR SCHOOL?
M.A.L.I.C.E. DOES HAVE A PENCHANT FOR TRIANGLE SYMBOLISM. THEIR UNIFORMS. THEIR HIDDEN BASE IN BERMUDA. EVEN OUR GEOMETRY HOMEWORK.
M.A.L.I.C.E. STANDS FOR MASTERMINDS ACTING LAWLESSLY IN COMMITTING EVIL.
BUT WHAT ABOUT "BALANCE?"
BIG ARCHENEMY LURKING ALWAYS NEAR THE CAFETERIA EMINENTLY!

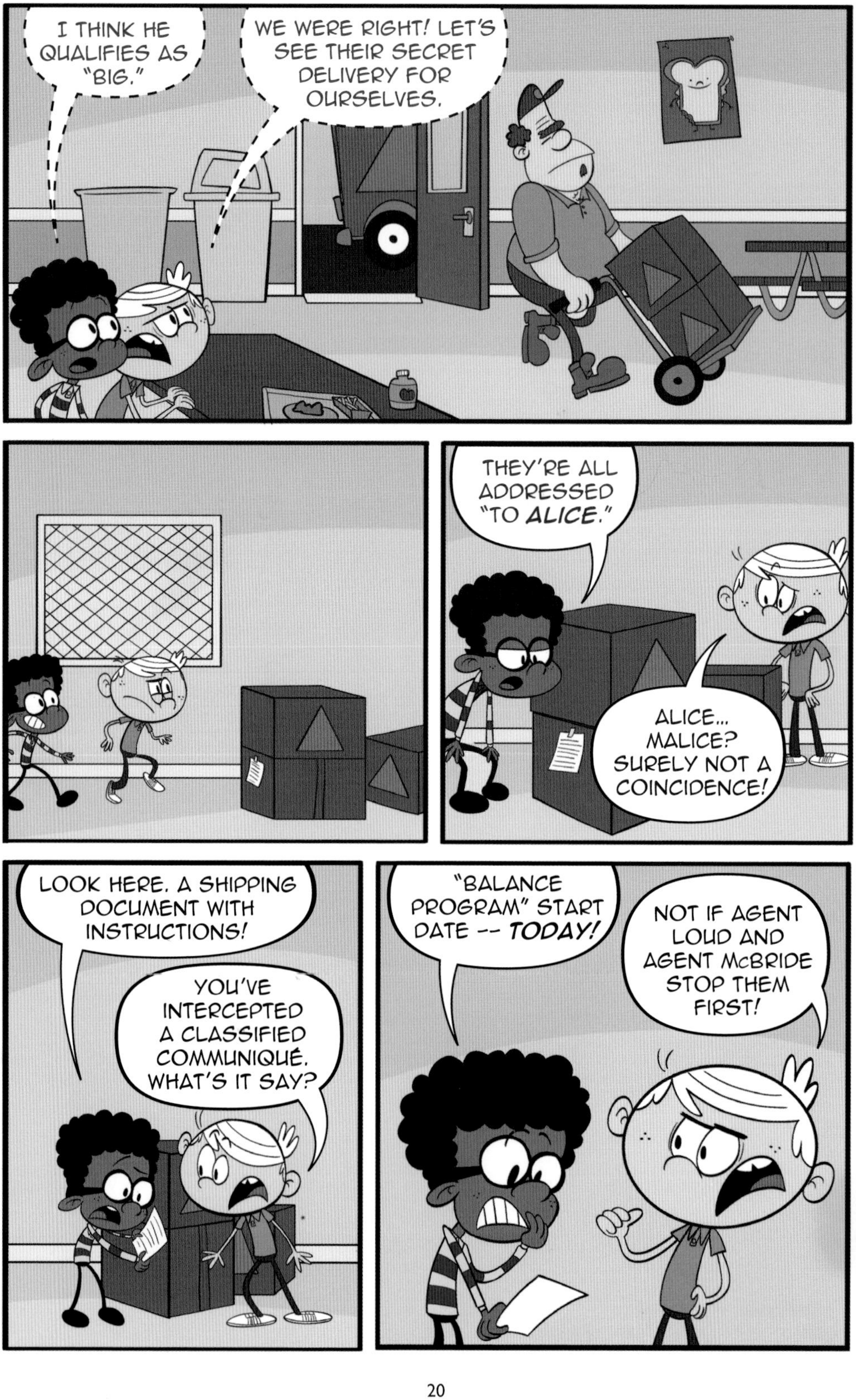
I THINK HE QUALIFIES AS "BIG."
WE WERE RIGHT! LET'S SEE THEIR SECRET DELIVERY FOR OURSELVES.
THEY'RE ALL ADDRESSED "TO *ALICE*."
ALICE... MALICE? SURELY NOT A COINCIDENCE!
LOOK HERE. A SHIPPING DOCUMENT WITH INSTRUCTIONS!
YOU'VE INTERCEPTED A CLASSIFIED COMMUNIQUÉ. WHAT'S IT SAY?
"BALANCE PROGRAM" START DATE -- *TODAY!*
NOT IF AGENT LOUD AND AGENT McBRIDE STOP THEM FIRST!

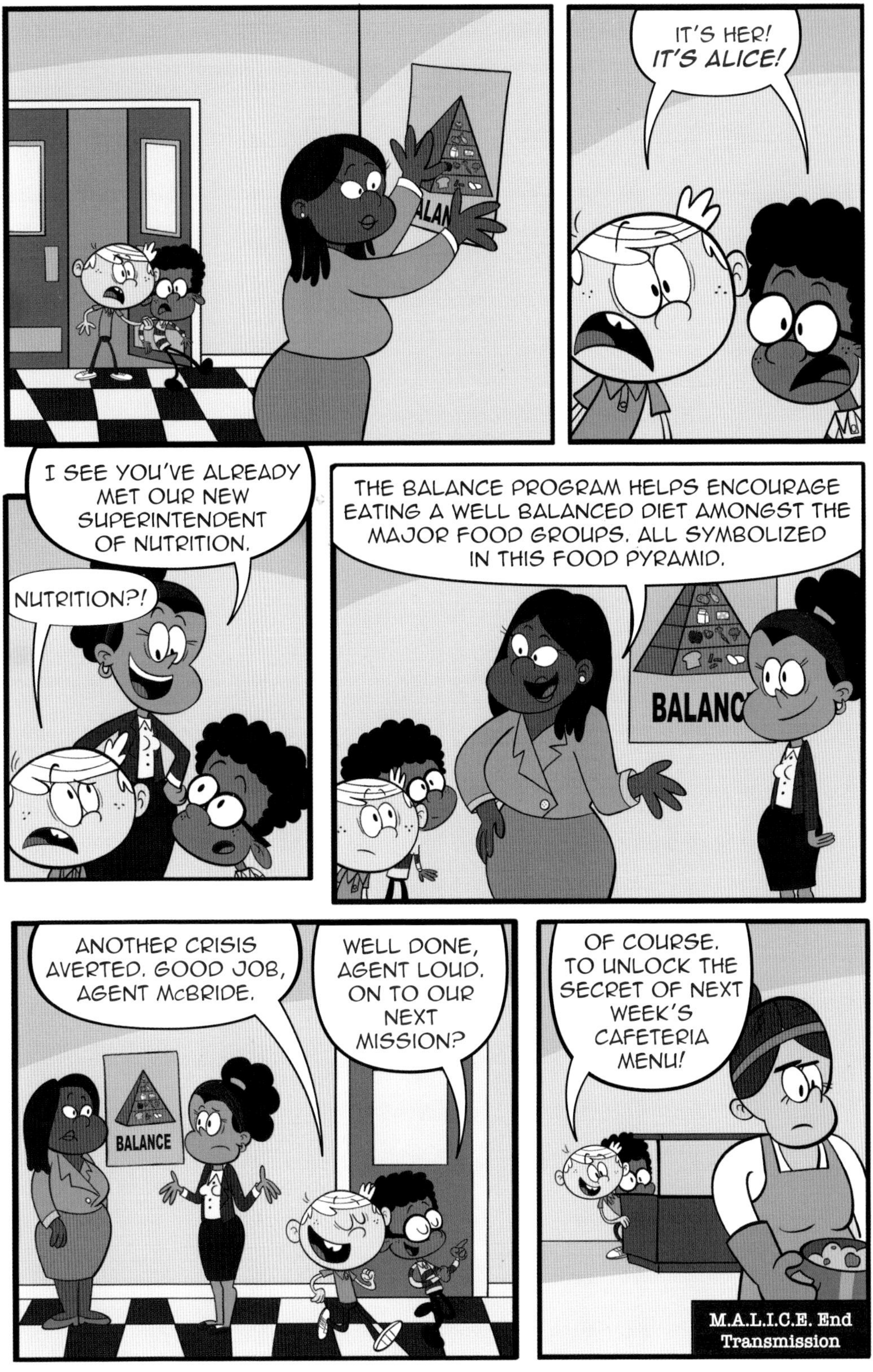
BALAN
IT'S HER!
IT'S ALICE!
I SEE YOU'VE ALREADY MET OUR NEW SUPERINTENDENT OF NUTRITION.
NUTRITION?!
THE BALANCE PROGRAM HELPS ENCOURAGE EATING A WELL BALANCED DIET AMONGST THE MAJOR FOOD GROUPS. ALL SYMBOLIZED IN THIS FOOD PYRAMID.
BALANC
ANOTHER CRISIS AVERTED. GOOD JOB, AGENT McBRIDE.
WELL DONE, AGENT LOUD. ON TO OUR NEXT MISSION?
BALANCE
OF COURSE. TO UNLOCK THE SECRET OF NEXT WEEK'S CAFETERIA MENU!
M.A.L.I.C.E. End Transmission

“ [illegible]I END[illegible] HIP [illegible]RAC[illegible] W[illegible]AT[illegible] ”

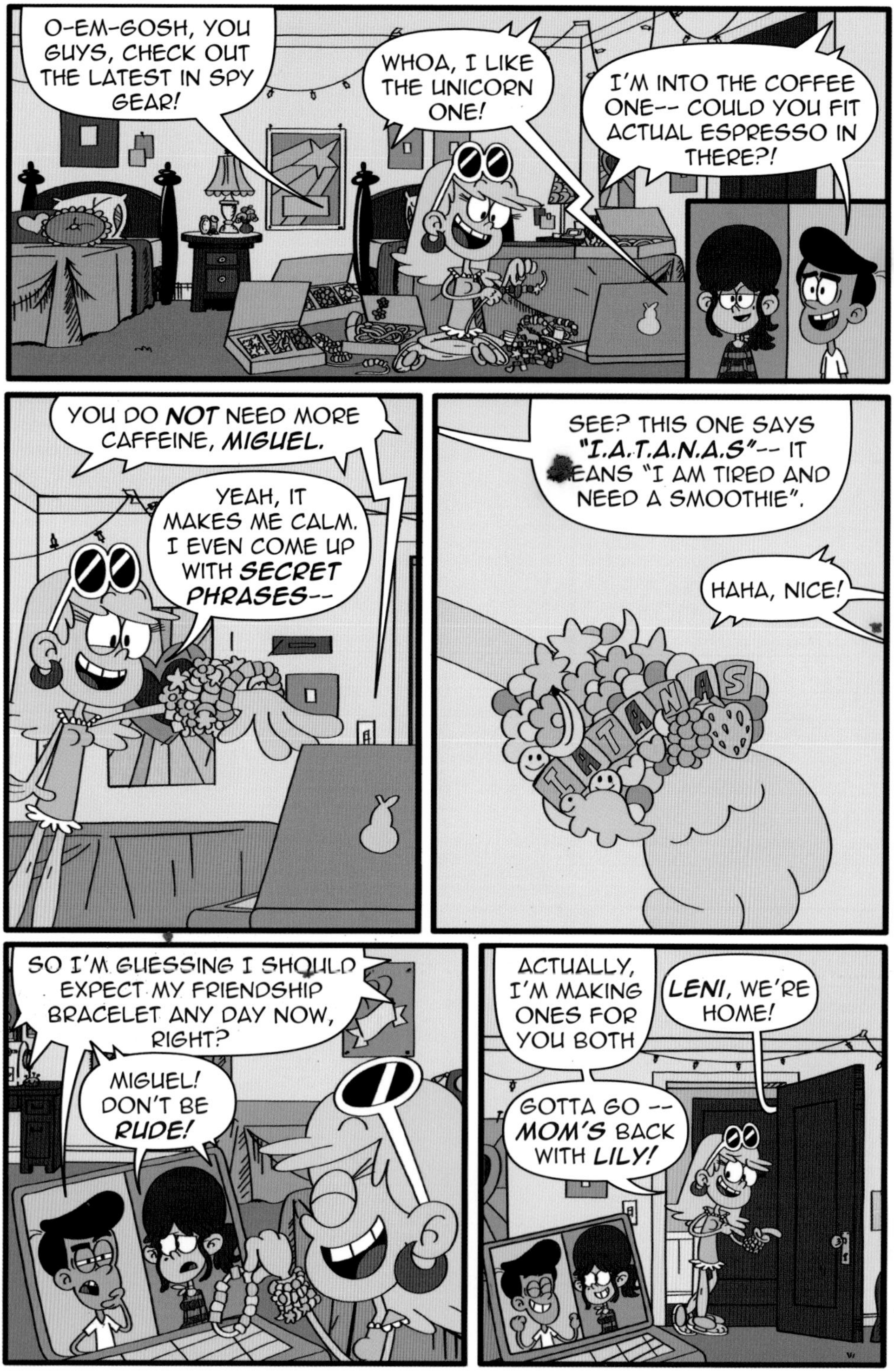

O-EM-GOSH, YOU GUYS, CHECK OUT THE LATEST IN SPY GEAR!
WHOA, I LIKE THE UNICORN ONE!
I'M INTO THE COFFEE ONE-- COULD YOU FIT ACTUAL ESPRESSO IN THERE?!
YOU DO NOT NEED MORE CAFFEINE, MIGUEL.
YEAH, IT MAKES ME CALM. I EVEN COME UP WITH SECRET PHRASES--
SEE? THIS ONE SAYS "I.A.T.A.N.A.S"-- IT MEANS "I AM TIRED AND NEED A SMOOTHIE".
HAHA, NICE!
IATANAS
SO I'M GUESSING I SHOULD EXPECT MY FRIENDSHIP BRACELET ANY DAY NOW, RIGHT?
MIGUEL! DON'T BE RUDE!
ACTUALLY, I'M MAKING ONES FOR YOU BOTH
LENI, WE'RE HOME!
GOTTA GO -- MOM'S BACK WITH LILY!

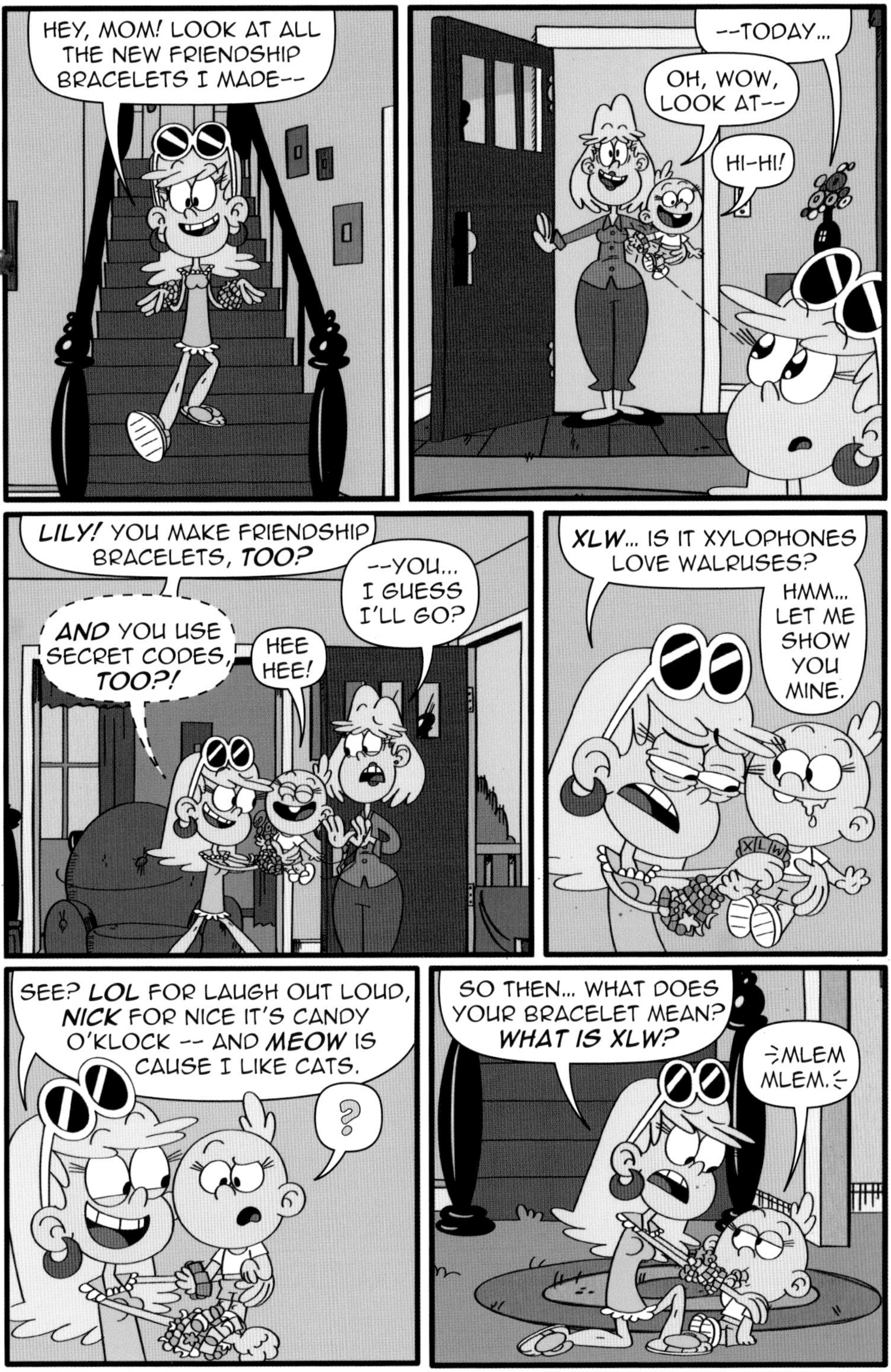
HEY, MOM! LOOK AT ALL THE NEW FRIENDSHIP BRACELETS I MADE--
--TODAY...
OH, WOW, LOOK AT--
HI-HI!
LILY! YOU MAKE FRIENDSHIP BRACELETS, TOO?
AND YOU USE SECRET CODES, TOO?!
HEE HEE!
--YOU... I GUESS I'LL GO?
XLW... IS IT XYLOPHONES LOVE WALRUSES?
HMM... LET ME SHOW YOU MINE.
XLW
SEE? LOL FOR LAUGH OUT LOUD, NICK FOR NICE IT'S CANDY O'KLOCK -- AND MEOW IS CAUSE I LIKE CATS.
?
SO THEN... WHAT DOES YOUR BRACELET MEAN? WHAT IS XLW?
MLEM MLEM.

THEN THERE'S ONLY ONE LOUD TO GO TO.

THIS IS JUST BABY-TALK.

NO WAY.

LILY TOLD ME IT MEANT MORE THAN THAT... OR, AT LEAST, IMPLIED IT.

YEAH!

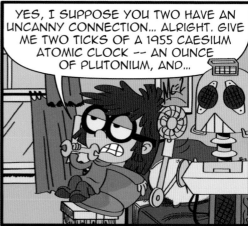

YES, I SUPPOSE YOU TWO HAVE AN UNCANNY CONNECTION... ALRIGHT. GIVE ME TWO TICKS OF A 1955 CAESIUM ATOMIC CLOCK -- AN OUNCE OF PLUTONIUM, AND...

MORE PLUTONIUM?

YES, YES, *DOUBLE IT.*

I DON'T KNOW, *LISA*... I DON'T THINK YOU'RE REALLY UNDERSTANDING THE POINT OF ALL THIS.

WHAT COULD YOU POSSIBLY MEAN?

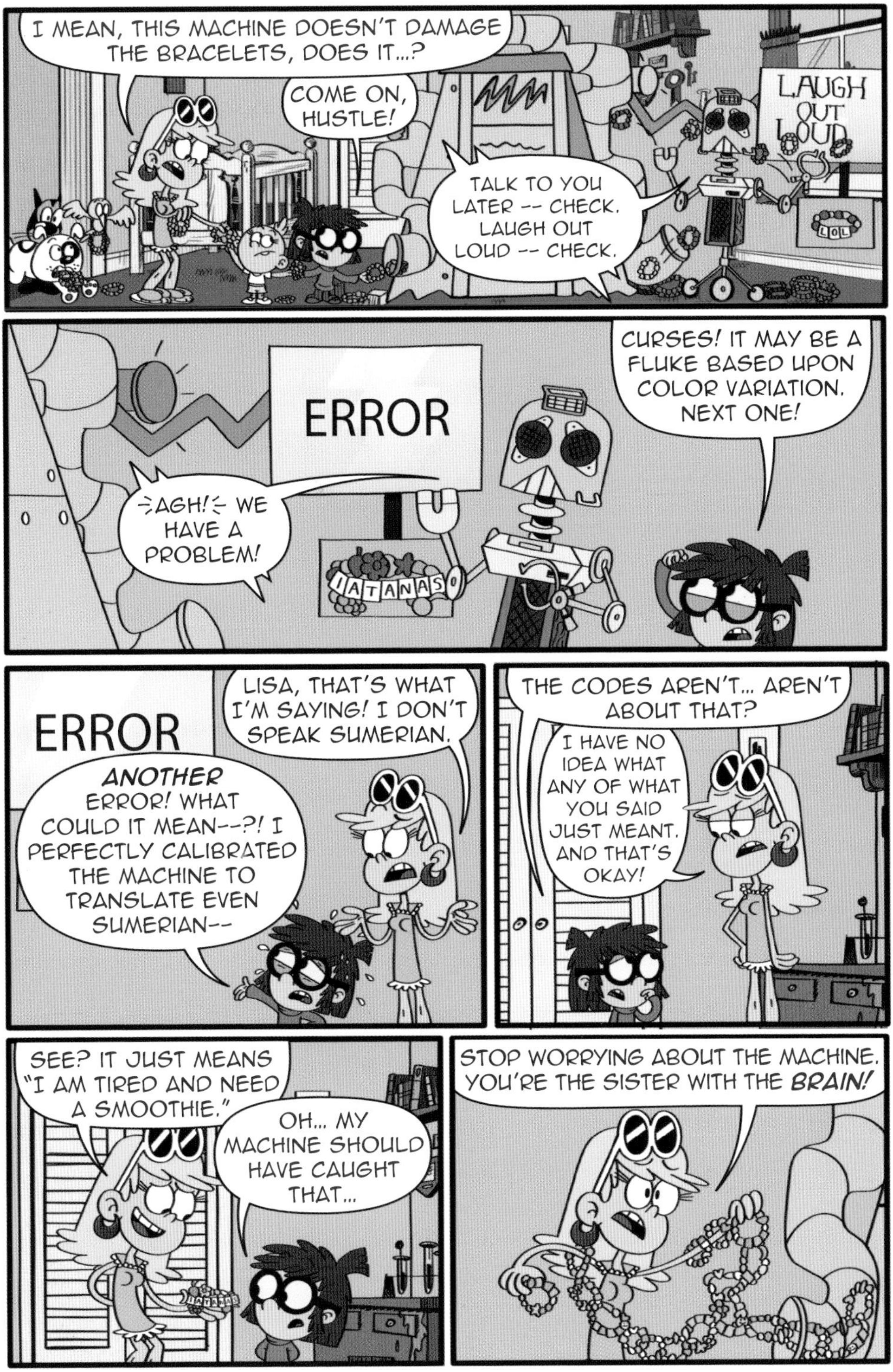
I MEAN, THIS MACHINE DOESN'T DAMAGE THE BRACELETS, DOES IT...?
COME ON, HUSTLE!
TALK TO YOU LATER -- CHECK. LAUGH OUT LOUD -- CHECK.
LAUGH OUT LOUD
LOL
ERROR
CURSES! IT MAY BE A FLUKE BASED UPON COLOR VARIATION. NEXT ONE!
AGH! WE HAVE A PROBLEM!
IATANAS
ERROR
LISA, THAT'S WHAT I'M SAYING! I DON'T SPEAK SUMERIAN.
ANOTHER ERROR! WHAT COULD IT MEAN--?! I PERFECTLY CALIBRATED THE MACHINE TO TRANSLATE EVEN SUMERIAN--
THE CODES AREN'T... AREN'T ABOUT THAT?
I HAVE NO IDEA WHAT ANY OF WHAT YOU SAID JUST MEANT. AND THAT'S OKAY!
SEE? IT JUST MEANS "I AM TIRED AND NEED A SMOOTHIE."
OH... MY MACHINE SHOULD HAVE CAUGHT THAT...
STOP WORRYING ABOUT THE MACHINE. YOU'RE THE SISTER WITH THE BRAIN!

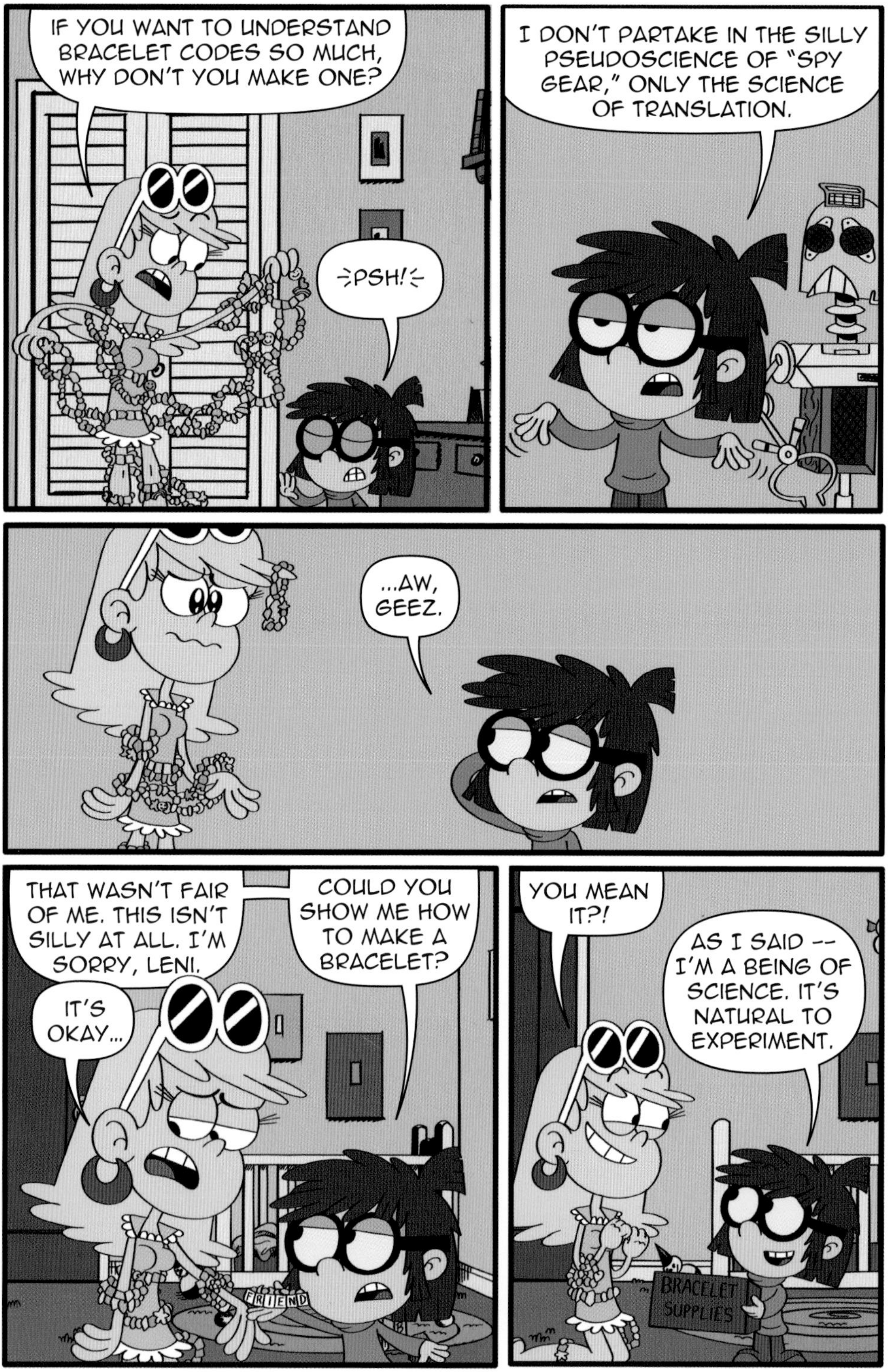
IF YOU WANT TO UNDERSTAND BRACELET CODES SO MUCH, WHY DON'T YOU MAKE ONE?
PSH!
I DON'T PARTAKE IN THE SILLY PSEUDOSCIENCE OF "SPY GEAR," ONLY THE SCIENCE OF TRANSLATION.
...AW, GEEZ.
THAT WASN'T FAIR OF ME. THIS ISN'T SILLY AT ALL. I'M SORRY, LENI.
COULD YOU SHOW ME HOW TO MAKE A BRACELET?
IT'S OKAY...
FRIEND
YOU MEAN IT?!
AS I SAID -- I'M A BEING OF SCIENCE. IT'S NATURAL TO EXPERIMENT.
BRACELET SUPPLIES

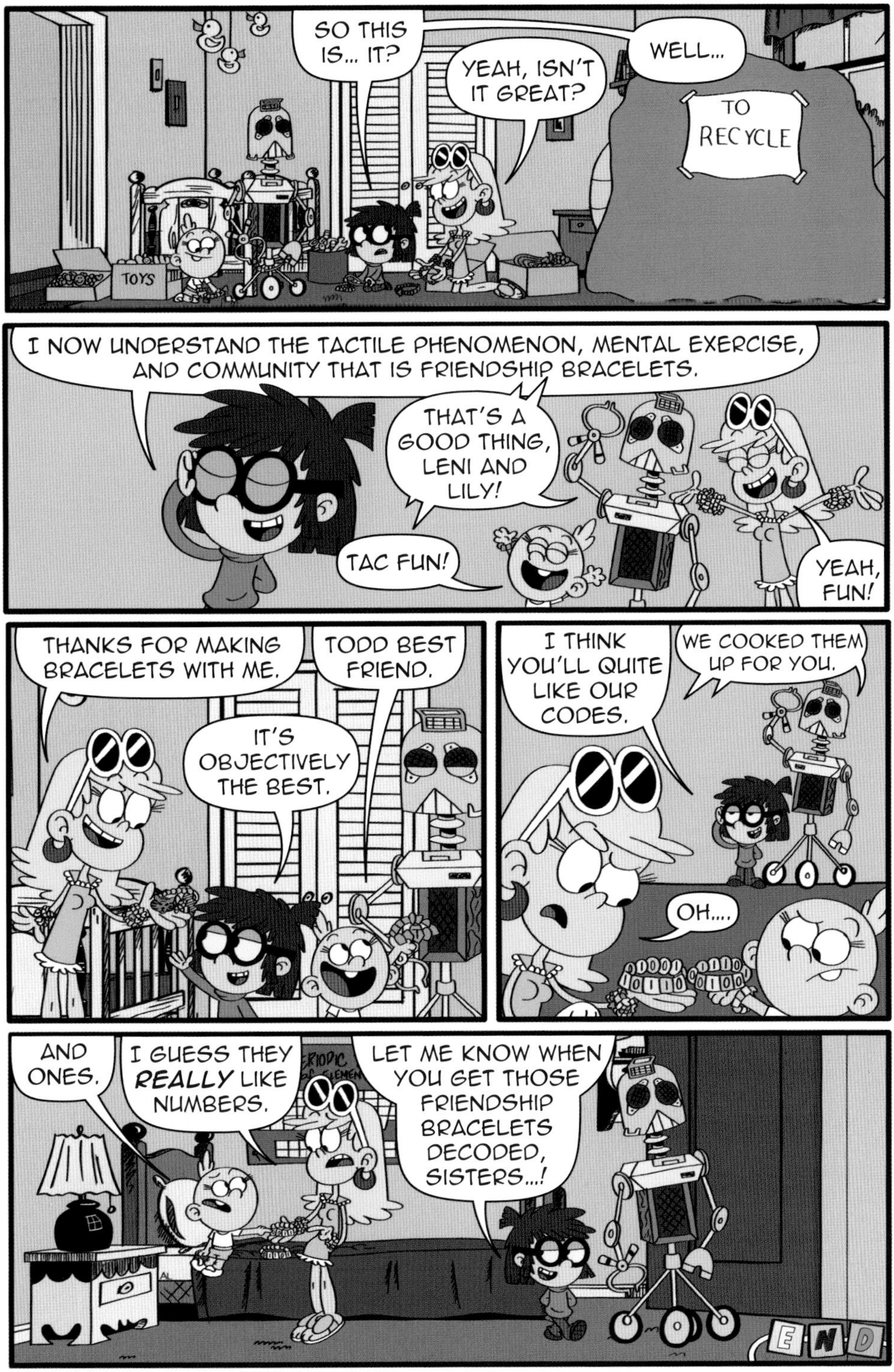
SO THIS IS... IT?
YEAH, ISN'T IT GREAT?
WELL...
TO RECYCLE
TOYS
I NOW UNDERSTAND THE TACTILE PHENOMENON, MENTAL EXERCISE, AND COMMUNITY THAT IS FRIENDSHIP BRACELETS.
THAT'S A GOOD THING, LENI AND LILY!
TAC FUN!
YEAH, FUN!
THANKS FOR MAKING BRACELETS WITH ME.
TODD BEST FRIEND.
IT'S OBJECTIVELY THE BEST.
I THINK YOU'LL QUITE LIKE OUR CODES.
WE COOKED THEM UP FOR YOU.
OH....
AND ONES.
I GUESS THEY *REALLY* LIKE NUMBERS.
LET ME KNOW WHEN YOU GET THOSE FRIENDSHIP BRACELETS DECODED, SISTERS...!
END

"SNEAK PEEK"

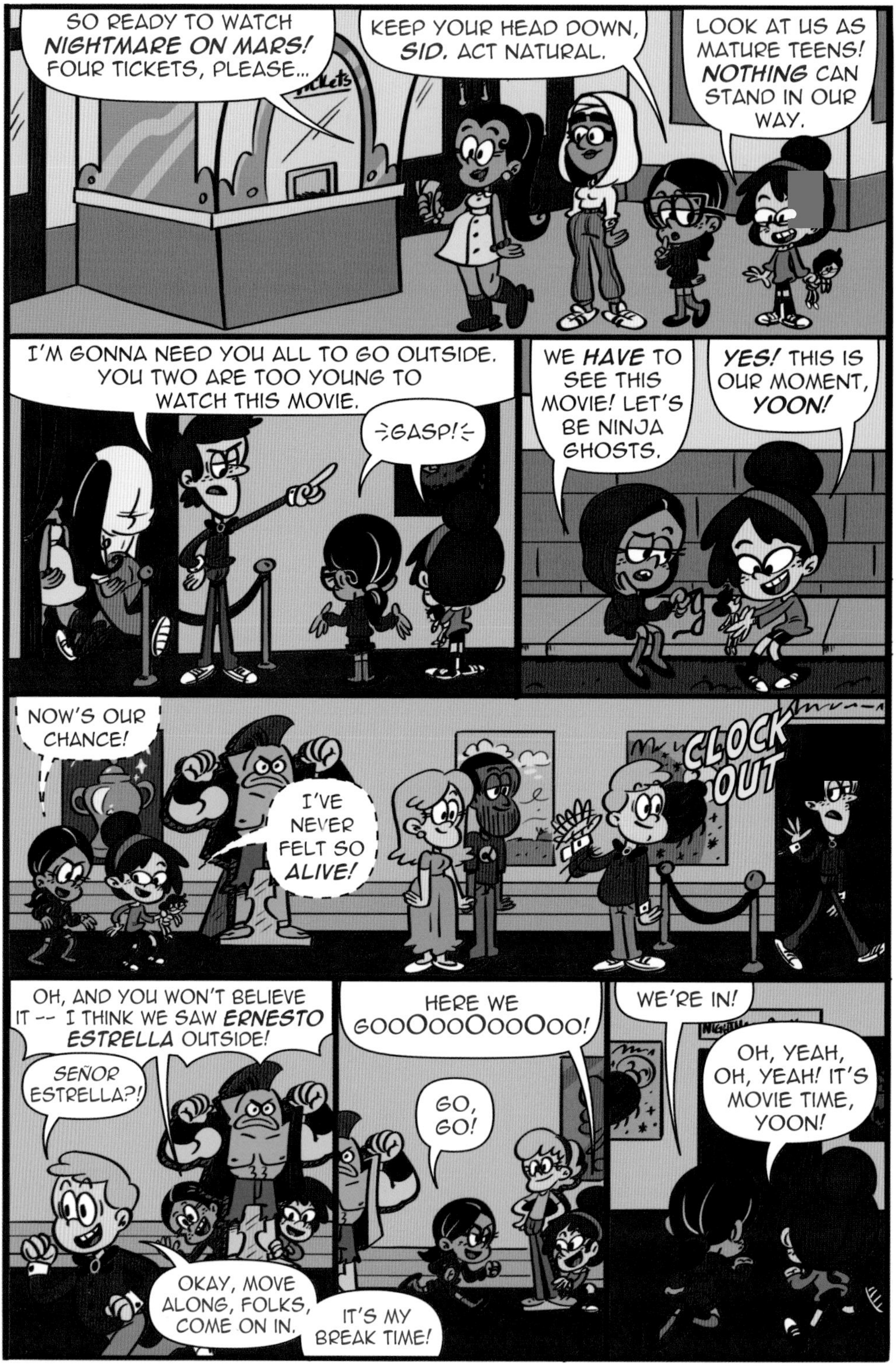
SO READY TO WATCH *NIGHTMARE ON MARS!* FOUR TICKETS, PLEASE...
TICKETS
KEEP YOUR HEAD DOWN, *SID.* ACT NATURAL.
LOOK AT US AS MATURE TEENS! *NOTHING* CAN STAND IN OUR WAY.
I'M GONNA NEED YOU ALL TO GO OUTSIDE. YOU TWO ARE TOO YOUNG TO WATCH THIS MOVIE.
GASP!
WE *HAVE* TO SEE THIS MOVIE! LET'S BE NINJA GHOSTS.
YES! THIS IS OUR MOMENT, *YOON!*
NOW'S OUR CHANCE!
I'VE NEVER FELT SO *ALIVE!*
CLOCK OUT
OH, AND YOU WON'T BELIEVE IT -- I THINK WE SAW *ERNESTO ESTRELLA* OUTSIDE!
SEÑOR ESTRELLA?!
OKAY, MOVE ALONG, FOLKS, COME ON IN.
IT'S MY BREAK TIME!
HERE WE GOOOOOOOOOOOO!
GO, GO!
WE'RE IN!
OH, YEAH, OH, YEAH! IT'S MOVIE TIME, YOON!

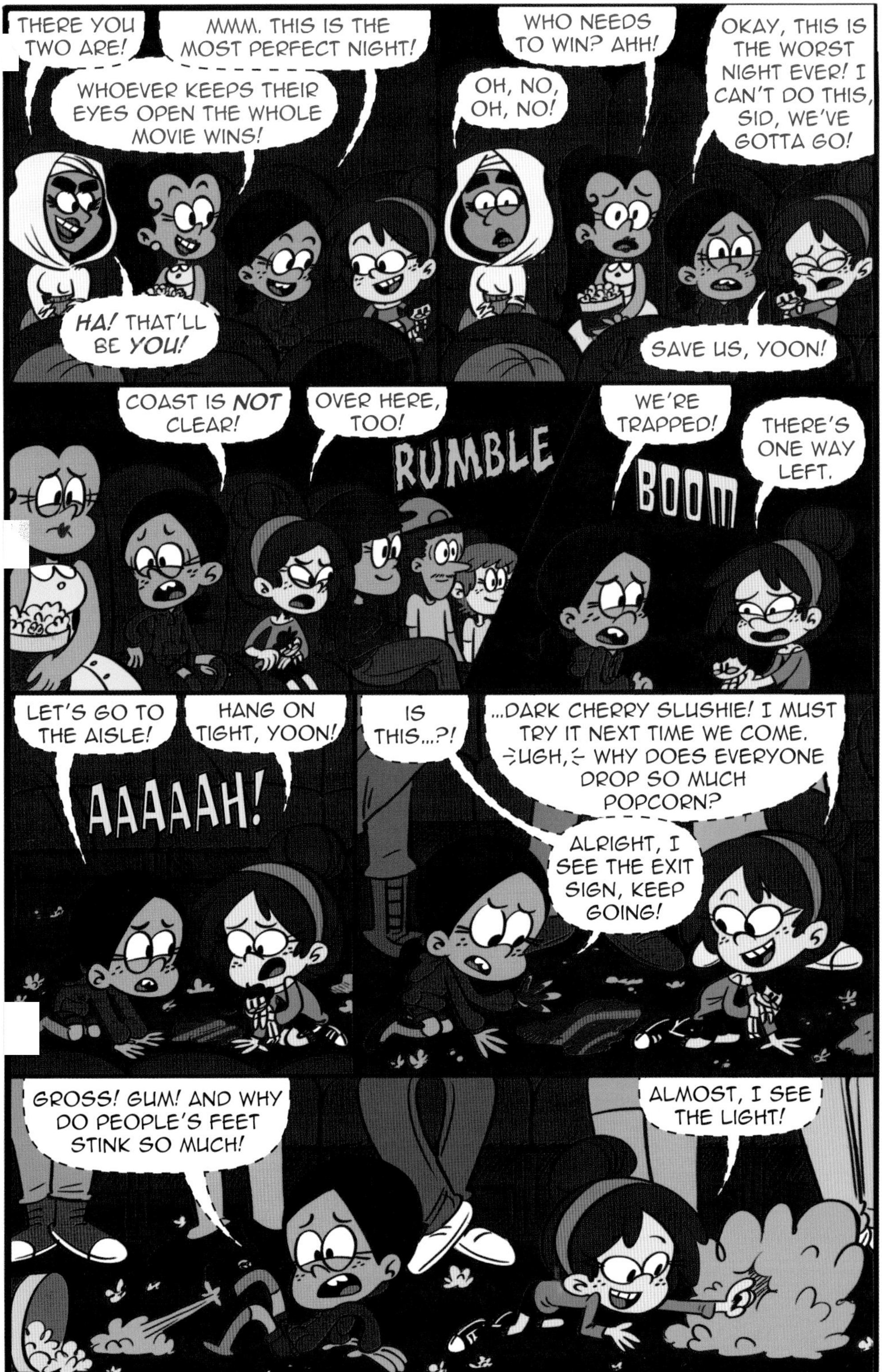
THERE YOU TWO ARE!
WHOEVER KEEPS THEIR EYES OPEN THE WHOLE MOVIE WINS!
MMM. THIS IS THE MOST PERFECT NIGHT!
HA! THAT'LL BE YOU!
WHO NEEDS TO WIN? AHH!
OH, NO, OH, NO!
OKAY, THIS IS THE WORST NIGHT EVER! I CAN'T DO THIS, SID, WE'VE GOTTA GO!
SAVE US, YOON!
COAST IS NOT CLEAR!
OVER HERE, TOO!
RUMBLE
WE'RE TRAPPED!
BOOM
THERE'S ONE WAY LEFT.
LET'S GO TO THE AISLE!
HANG ON TIGHT, YOON!
AAAAAH!
IS THIS...?!
...DARK CHERRY SLUSHIE! I MUST TRY IT NEXT TIME WE COME. UGH, WHY DOES EVERYONE DROP SO MUCH POPCORN?
ALRIGHT, I SEE THE EXIT SIGN, KEEP GOING!
GROSS! GUM! AND WHY DO PEOPLE'S FEET STINK SO MUCH!
ALMOST, I SEE THE LIGHT!

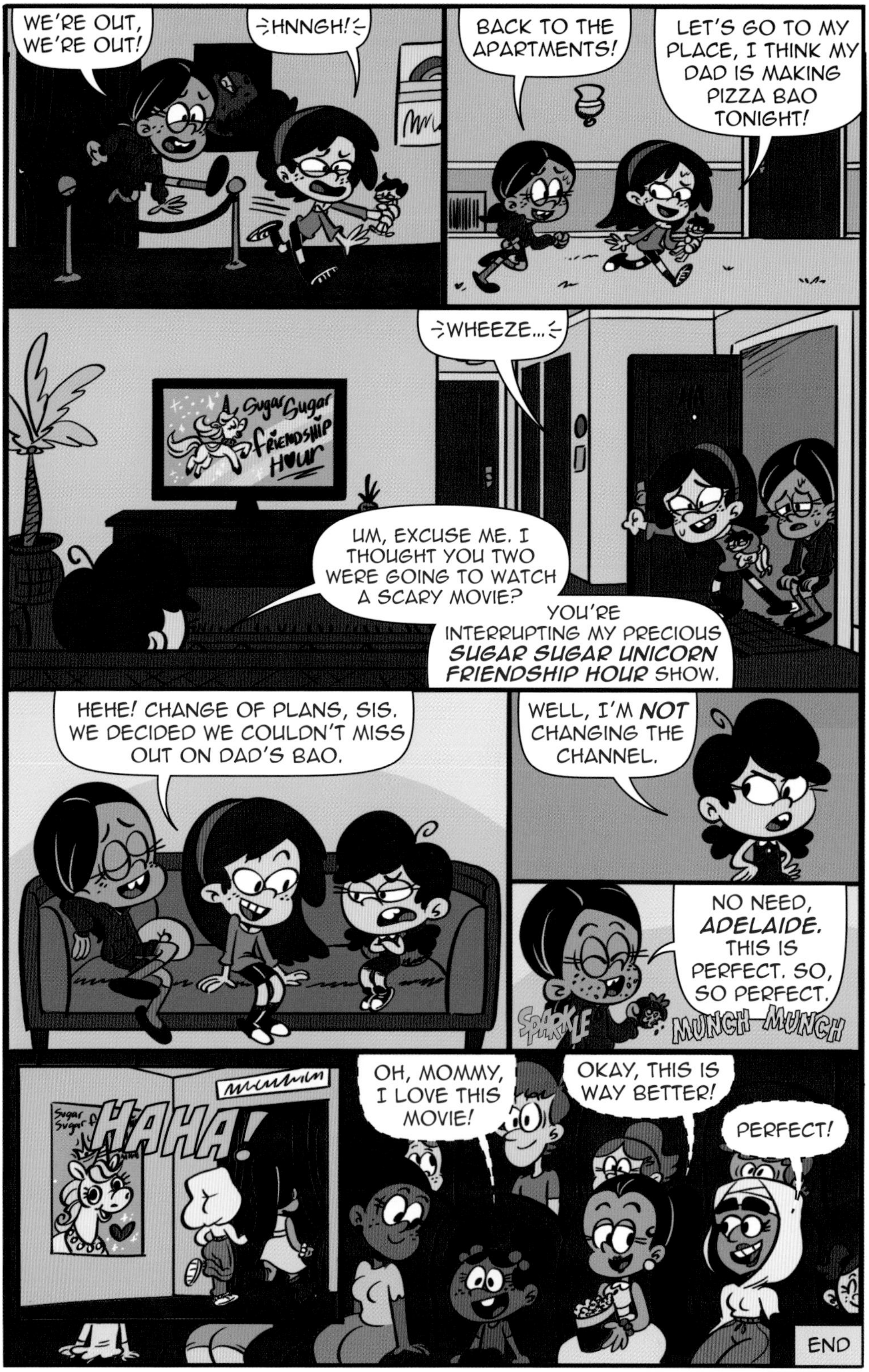
WE'RE OUT, WE'RE OUT!
HNNGH!
BACK TO THE APARTMENTS!
LET'S GO TO MY PLACE, I THINK MY DAD IS MAKING PIZZA BAO TONIGHT!
WHEEZE...
Sugar Sugar Friendship Hour
UM, EXCUSE ME. I THOUGHT YOU TWO WERE GOING TO WATCH A SCARY MOVIE?
YOU'RE INTERRUPTING MY PRECIOUS SUGAR SUGAR UNICORN FRIENDSHIP HOUR SHOW.
HEHE! CHANGE OF PLANS, SIS. WE DECIDED WE COULDN'T MISS OUT ON DAD'S BAO.
WELL, I'M NOT CHANGING THE CHANNEL.
NO NEED, ADELAIDE. THIS IS PERFECT. SO, SO PERFECT.
SPARKLE
MUNCH MUNCH
HAHA!
OH, MOMMY, I LOVE THIS MOVIE!
OKAY, THIS IS WAY BETTER!
PERFECT!
END

"OPERATION B.U.T.T"

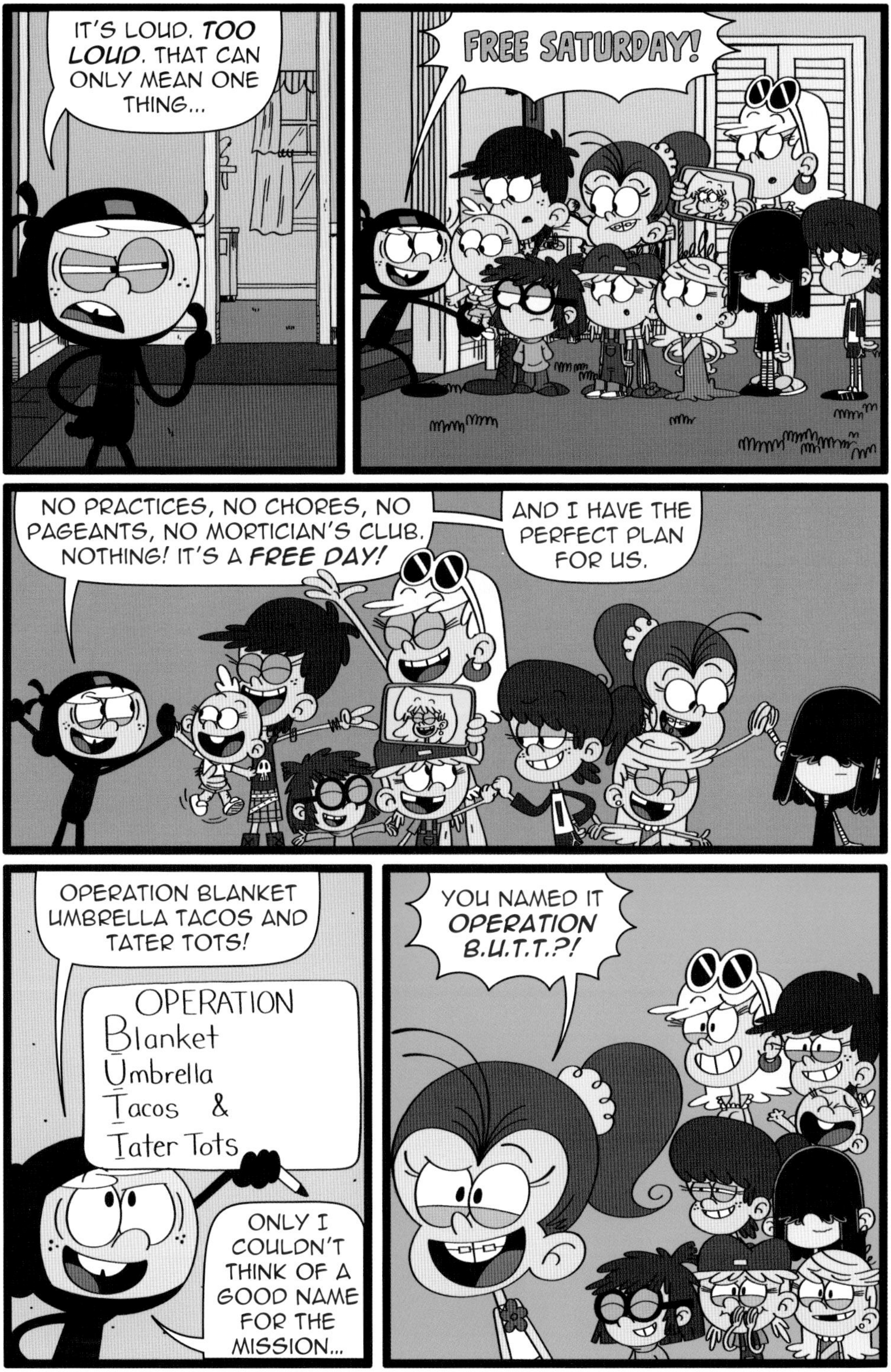
IT'S LOUD. *TOO LOUD*. THAT CAN ONLY MEAN ONE THING...
FREE SATURDAY!
NO PRACTICES, NO CHORES, NO PAGEANTS, NO MORTICIAN'S CLUB. NOTHING! IT'S A *FREE DAY!*
AND I HAVE THE PERFECT PLAN FOR US.
OPERATION BLANKET UMBRELLA TACOS AND TATER TOTS!
OPERATION
Blanket
Umbrella
Tacos &
Tater Tots
ONLY I COULDN'T THINK OF A GOOD NAME FOR THE MISSION...
YOU NAMED IT *OPERATION B.U.T.T.?!*

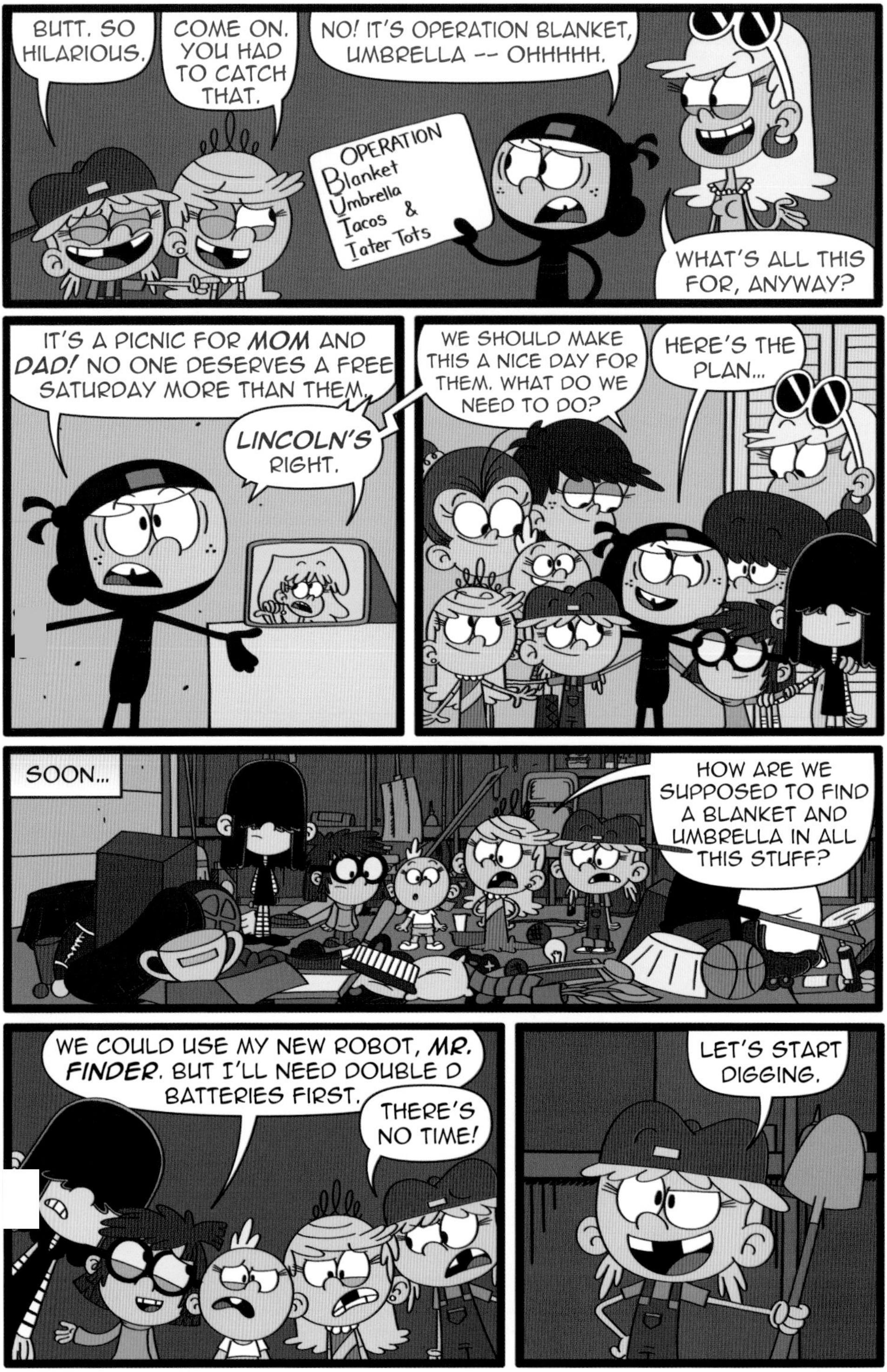
BUTT. SO HILARIOUS.
COME ON. YOU HAD TO CATCH THAT.
NO! IT'S OPERATION BLANKET, UMBRELLA -- OHHHHH.
OPERATION
Blanket
Umbrella
Tacos &
Tater Tots
WHAT'S ALL THIS FOR, ANYWAY?
IT'S A PICNIC FOR MOM AND DAD! NO ONE DESERVES A FREE SATURDAY MORE THAN THEM.
LINCOLN'S RIGHT.
WE SHOULD MAKE THIS A NICE DAY FOR THEM. WHAT DO WE NEED TO DO?
HERE'S THE PLAN...
SOON...
HOW ARE WE SUPPOSED TO FIND A BLANKET AND UMBRELLA IN ALL THIS STUFF?
WE COULD USE MY NEW ROBOT, MR. FINDER. BUT I'LL NEED DOUBLE D BATTERIES FIRST.
THERE'S NO TIME!
LET'S START DIGGING.

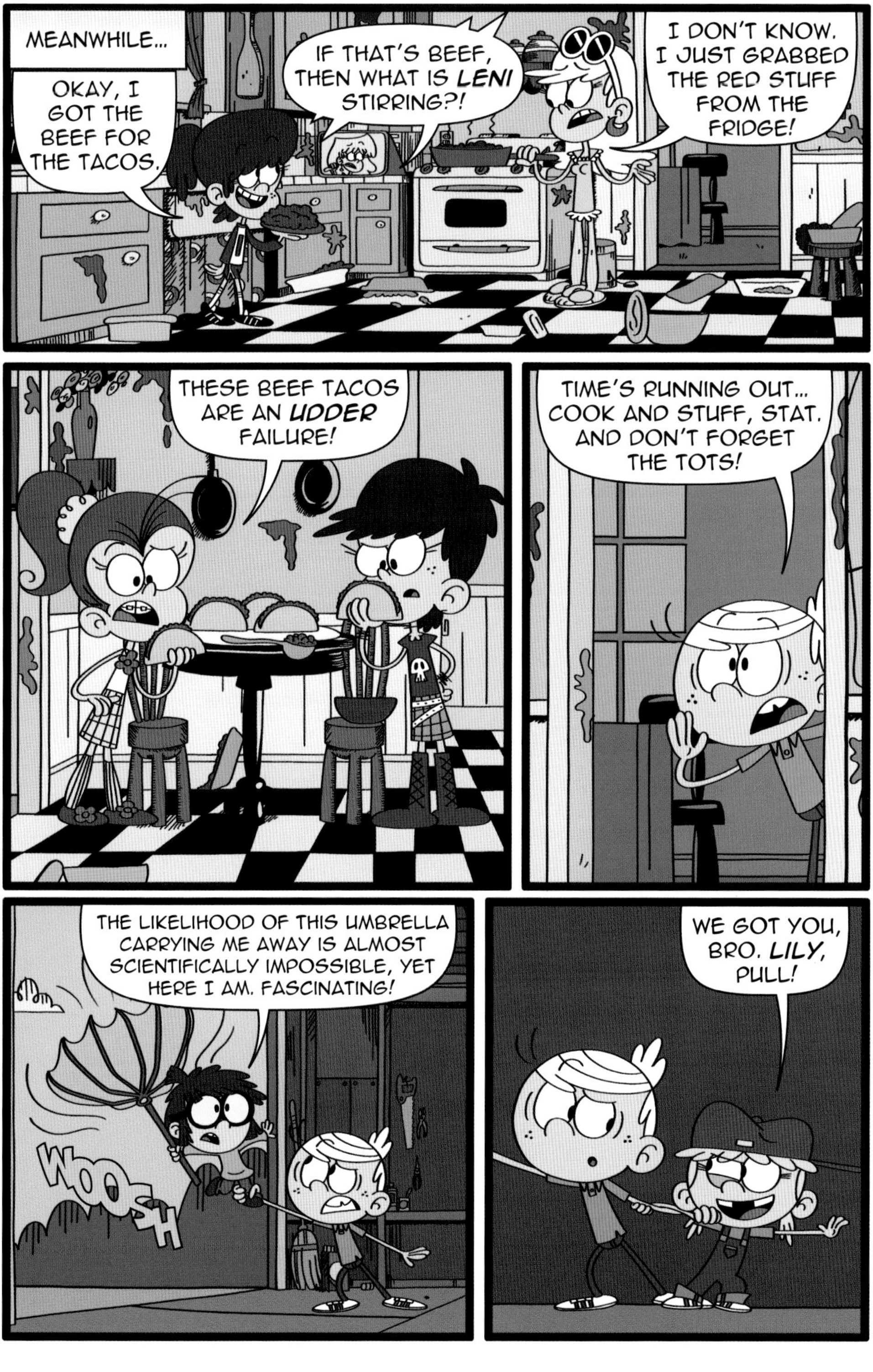
MEANWHILE...
OKAY, I GOT THE BEEF FOR THE TACOS.
IF THAT'S BEEF, THEN WHAT IS LENI STIRRING?!
I DON'T KNOW. I JUST GRABBED THE RED STUFF FROM THE FRIDGE!
THESE BEEF TACOS ARE AN UDDER FAILURE!
TIME'S RUNNING OUT... COOK AND STUFF, STAT. AND DON'T FORGET THE TOTS!
THE LIKELIHOOD OF THIS UMBRELLA CARRYING ME AWAY IS ALMOST SCIENTIFICALLY IMPOSSIBLE, YET HERE I AM. FASCINATING!
WOOSH
WE GOT YOU, BRO. LILY, PULL!

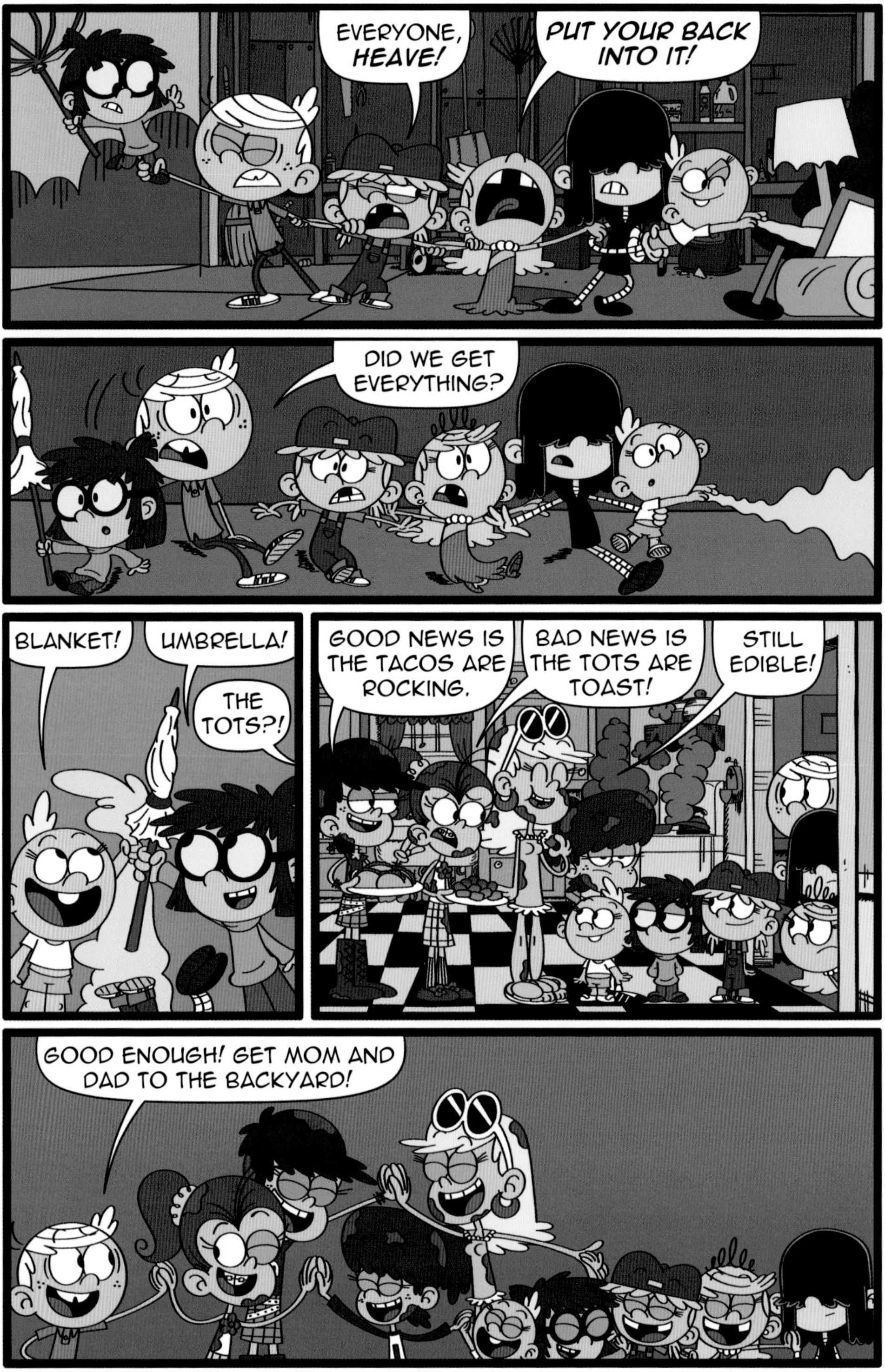
EVERYONE, HEAVE!
PUT YOUR BACK INTO IT!
DID WE GET EVERYTHING?
BLANKET!
UMBRELLA!
THE TOTS?!
GOOD NEWS IS THE TACOS ARE ROCKING.
BAD NEWS IS THE TOTS ARE TOAST!
STILL EDIBLE!
GOOD ENOUGH! GET MOM AND DAD TO THE BACKYARD!

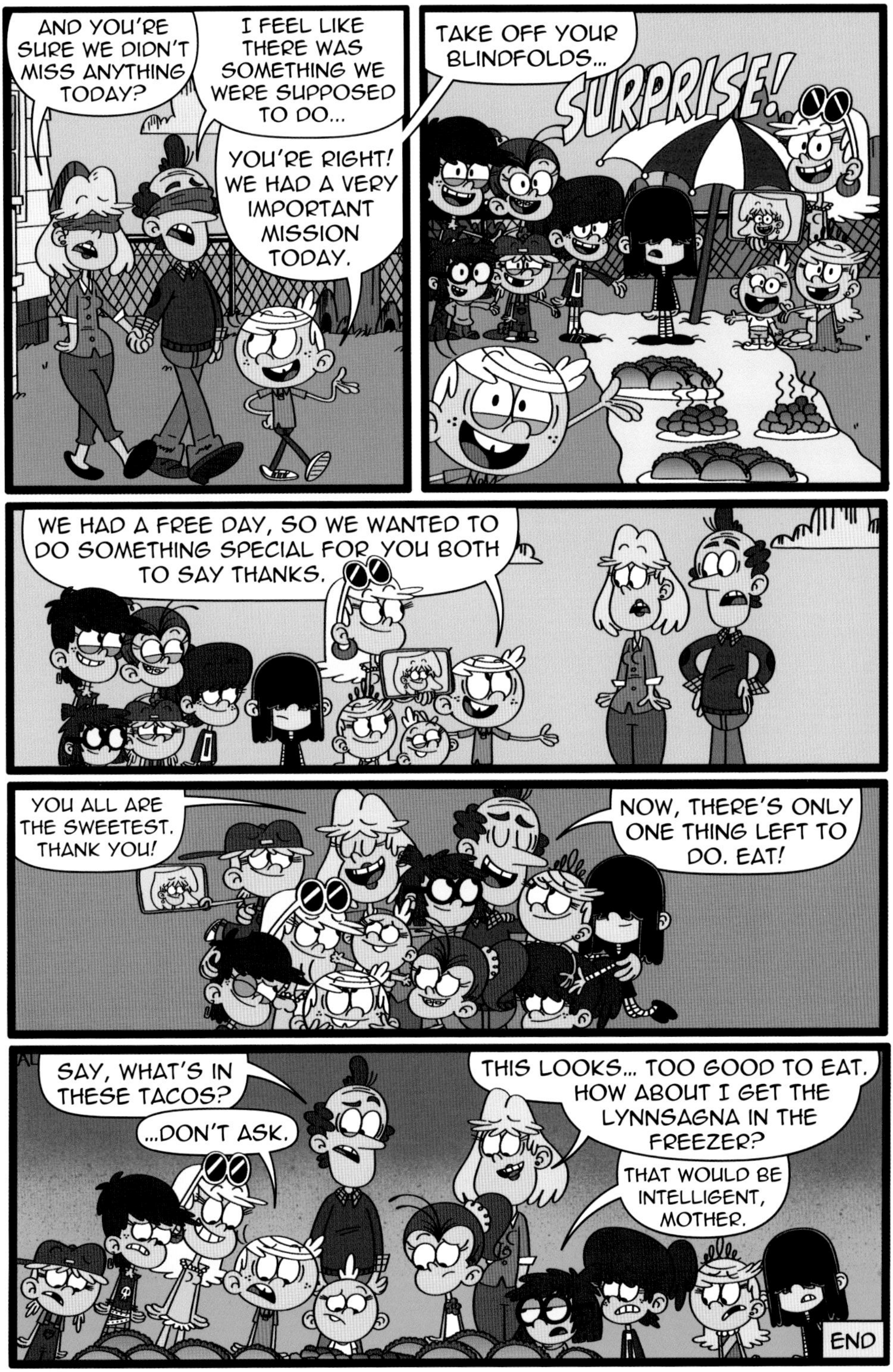
AND YOU'RE SURE WE DIDN'T MISS ANYTHING TODAY?
I FEEL LIKE THERE WAS SOMETHING WE WERE SUPPOSED TO DO...
YOU'RE RIGHT! WE HAD A VERY IMPORTANT MISSION TODAY.
TAKE OFF YOUR BLINDFOLDS...
SURPRISE!
WE HAD A FREE DAY, SO WE WANTED TO DO SOMETHING SPECIAL FOR YOU BOTH TO SAY THANKS.
YOU ALL ARE THE SWEETEST. THANK YOU!
NOW, THERE'S ONLY ONE THING LEFT TO DO. EAT!
SAY, WHAT'S IN THESE TACOS?
...DON'T ASK.
THIS LOOKS... TOO GOOD TO EAT. HOW ABOUT I GET THE LYNNSAGNA IN THE FREEZER?
THAT WOULD BE INTELLIGENT, MOTHER.
END

"STICKY FINGERS"

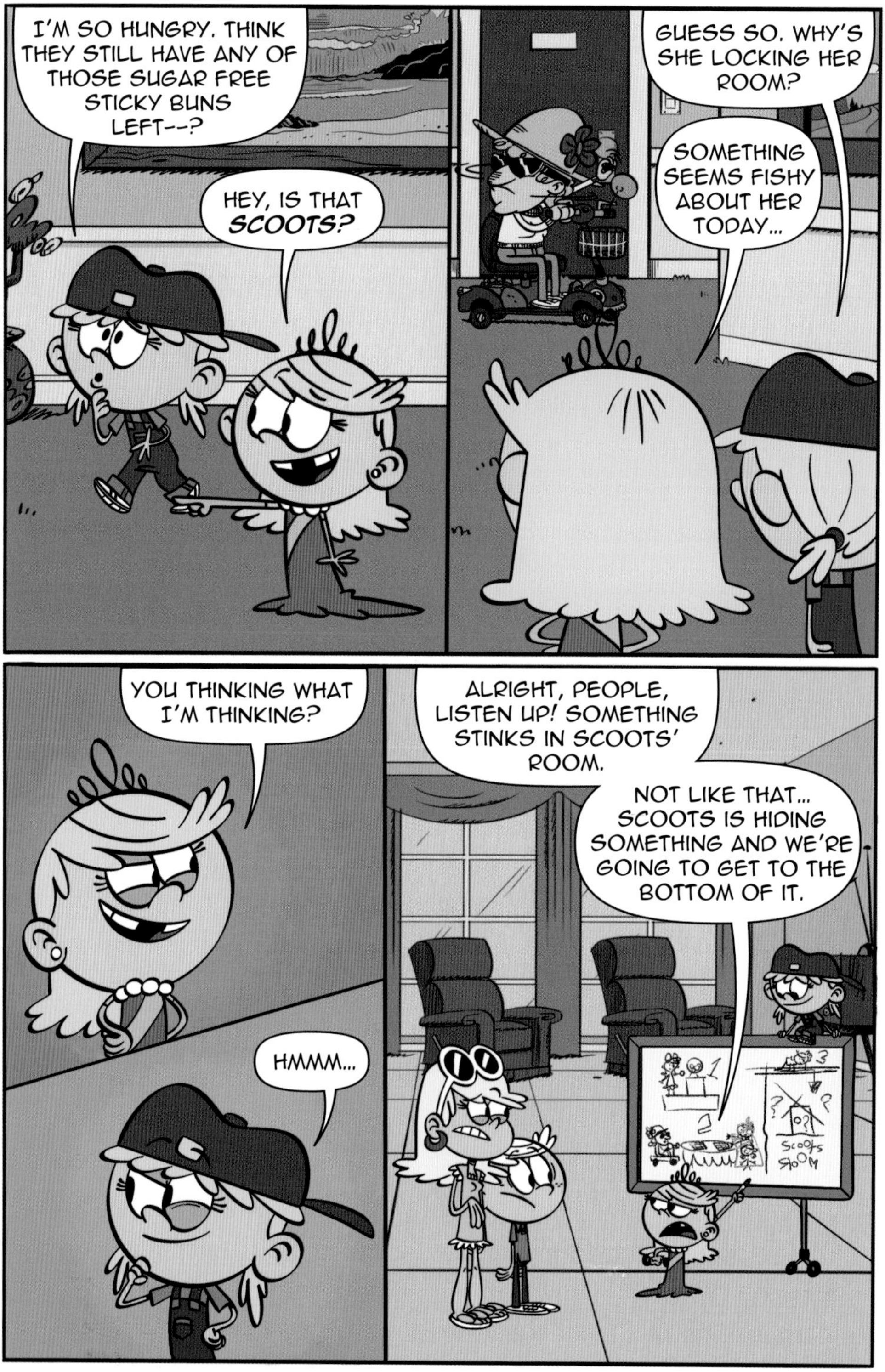

I'M SO HUNGRY. THINK THEY STILL HAVE ANY OF THOSE SUGAR FREE STICKY BUNS LEFT--?
HEY, IS THAT *SCOOTS?*
GUESS SO. WHY'S SHE LOCKING HER ROOM?
SOMETHING SEEMS FISHY ABOUT HER TODAY...
YOU THINKING WHAT I'M THINKING?
HMMM...
ALRIGHT, PEOPLE, LISTEN UP! SOMETHING STINKS IN SCOOTS' ROOM.
NOT LIKE THAT... SCOOTS IS HIDING SOMETHING AND WE'RE GOING TO GET TO THE BOTTOM OF IT.

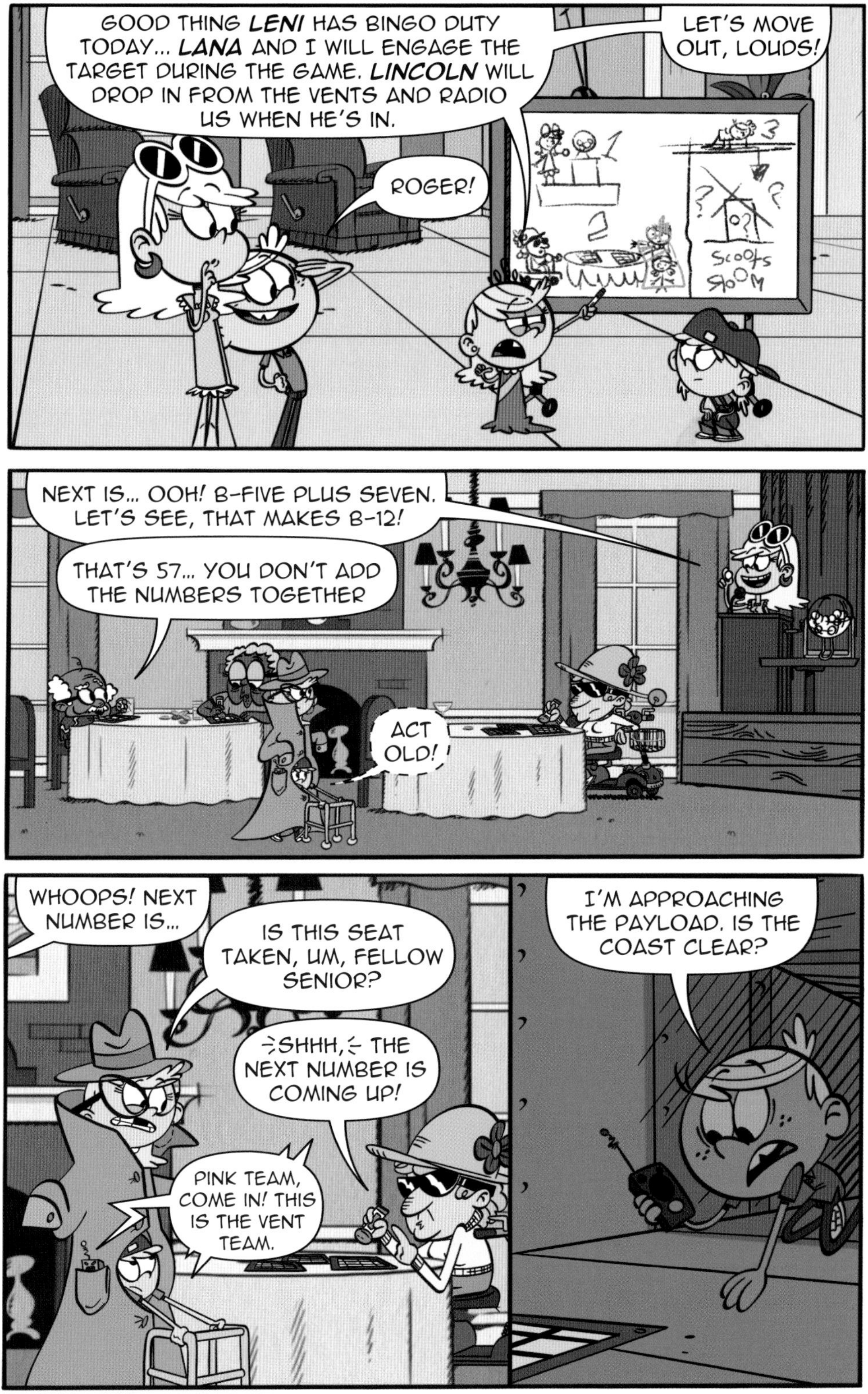
GOOD THING LENI HAS BINGO DUTY TODAY... LANA AND I WILL ENGAGE THE TARGET DURING THE GAME. LINCOLN WILL DROP IN FROM THE VENTS AND RADIO US WHEN HE'S IN.
LET'S MOVE OUT, LOUDS!
ROGER!
SCOOTS ROOM
NEXT IS... OOH! B-FIVE PLUS SEVEN. LET'S SEE, THAT MAKES B-12!
THAT'S 57... YOU DON'T ADD THE NUMBERS TOGETHER
ACT OLD!
WHOOPS! NEXT NUMBER IS...
IS THIS SEAT TAKEN, UM, FELLOW SENIOR?
SHHH, THE NEXT NUMBER IS COMING UP!
PINK TEAM, COME IN! THIS IS THE VENT TEAM.
I'M APPROACHING THE PAYLOAD. IS THE COAST CLEAR?

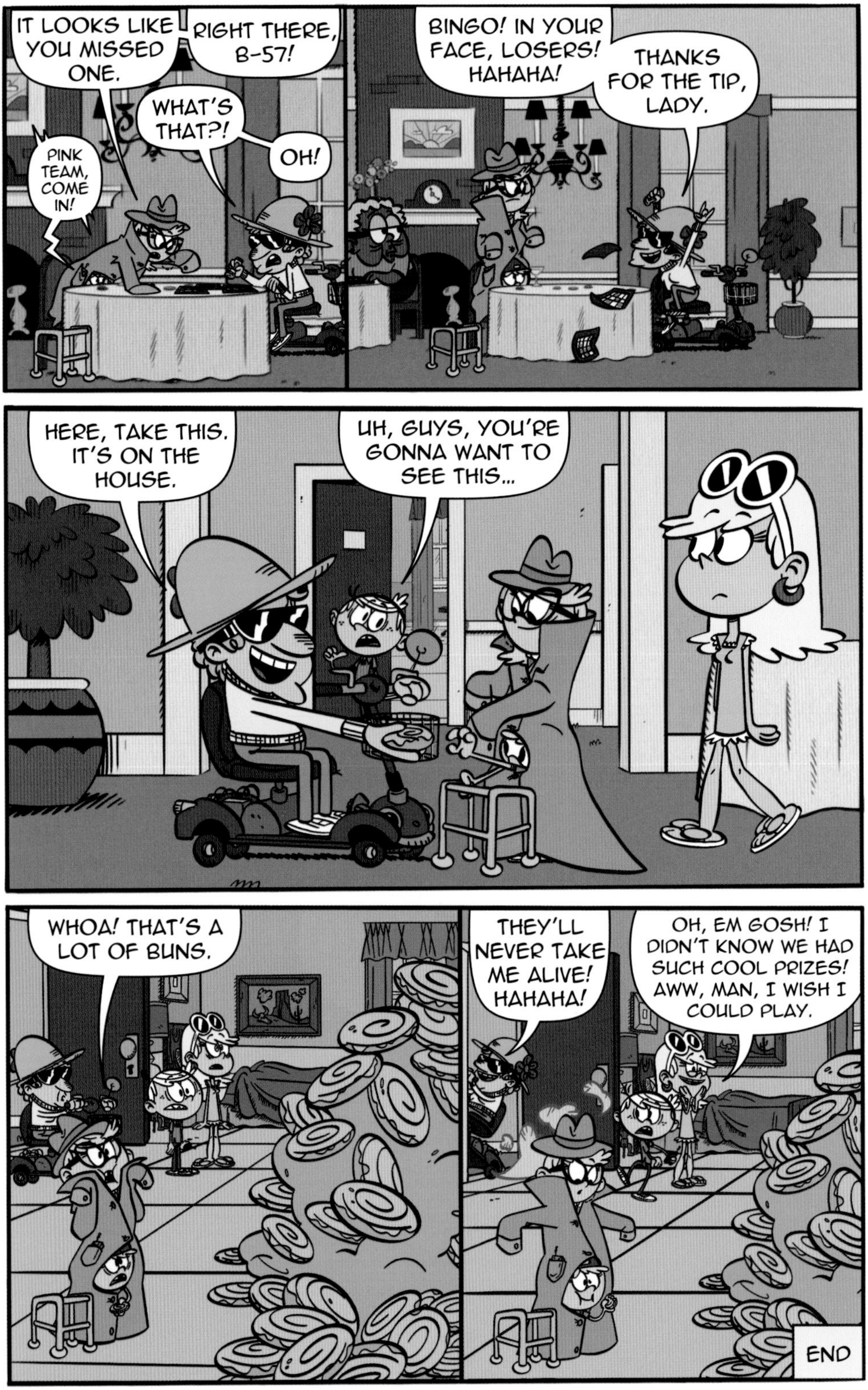
IT LOOKS LIKE YOU MISSED ONE.
RIGHT THERE, B-57!
PINK TEAM, COME IN!
WHAT'S THAT?!
OH!
BINGO! IN YOUR FACE, LOSERS! HAHAHA!
THANKS FOR THE TIP, LADY.
HERE, TAKE THIS. IT'S ON THE HOUSE.
UH, GUYS, YOU'RE GONNA WANT TO SEE THIS...
WHOA! THAT'S A LOT OF BUNS.
THEY'LL NEVER TAKE ME ALIVE! HAHAHA!
OH, EM GOSH! I DIDN'T KNOW WE HAD SUCH COOL PRIZES! AWW, MAN, I WISH I COULD PLAY.
END

"COCKROACH APPROACH"

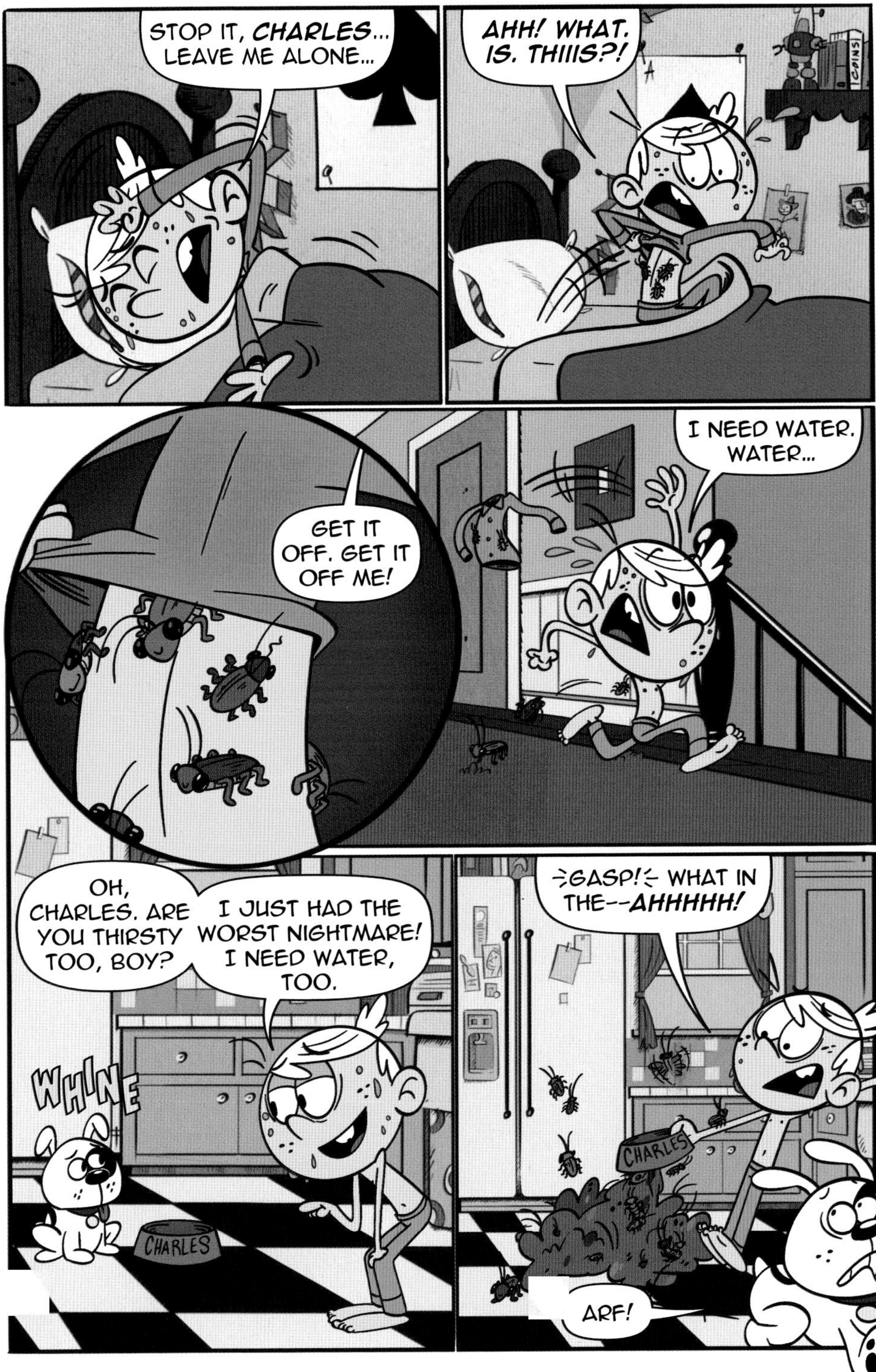
STOP IT, CHARLES... LEAVE ME ALONE...
AHH! WHAT. IS. THIIIS?!
COINS
GET IT OFF. GET IT OFF ME!
I NEED WATER. WATER...
OH, CHARLES. ARE YOU THIRSTY TOO, BOY?
I JUST HAD THE WORST NIGHTMARE! I NEED WATER, TOO.
WHINE
CHARLES
GASP! WHAT IN THE--AHHHHH!
CHARLES
ARF!

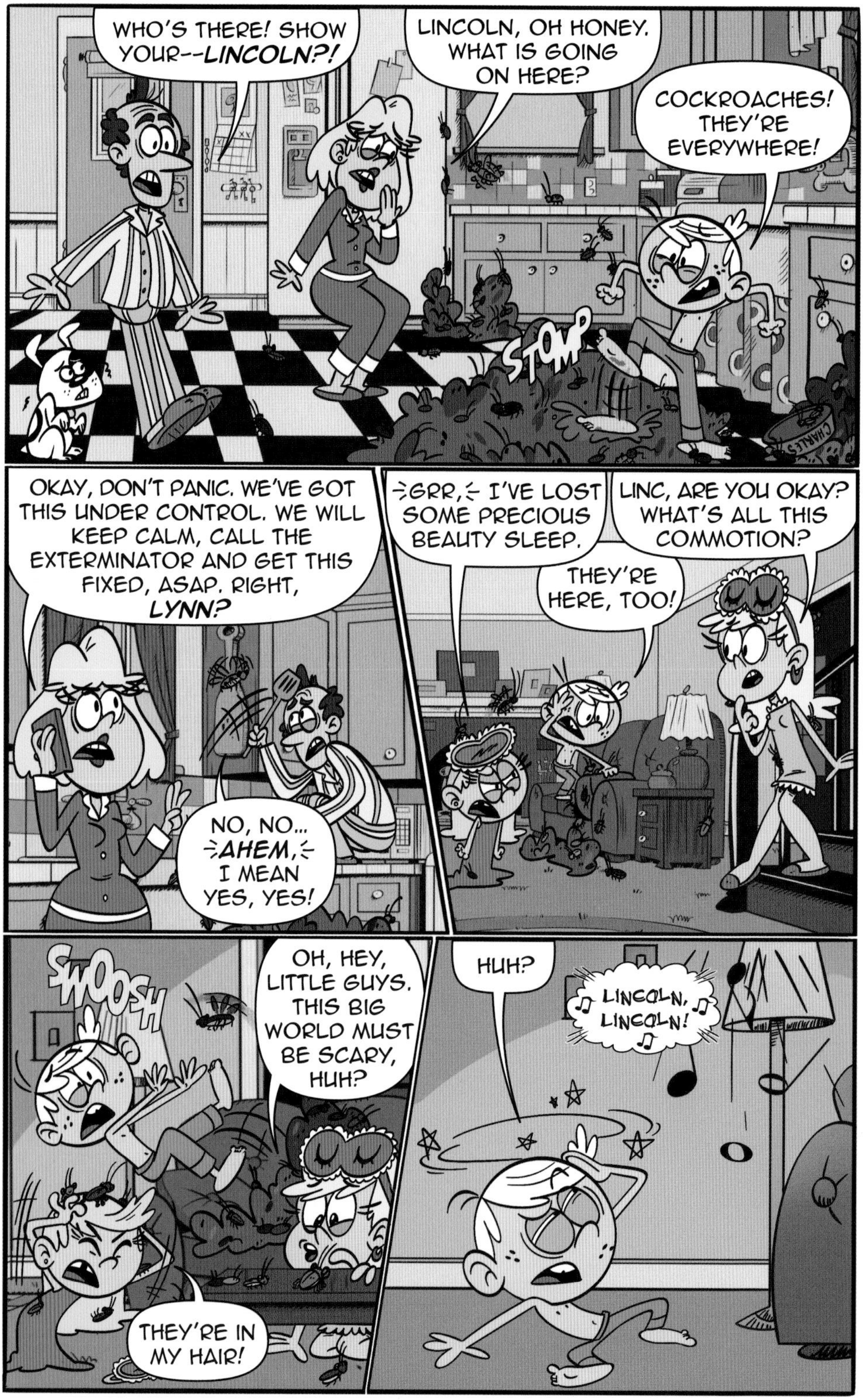
WHO'S THERE! SHOW YOUR--LINCOLN?!
LINCOLN, OH HONEY. WHAT IS GOING ON HERE?
COCKROACHES! THEY'RE EVERYWHERE!
STOMP
CHARLES
OKAY, DON'T PANIC. WE'VE GOT THIS UNDER CONTROL. WE WILL KEEP CALM, CALL THE EXTERMINATOR AND GET THIS FIXED, ASAP. RIGHT, LYNN?
NO, NO... AHEM, I MEAN YES, YES!
GRR, I'VE LOST SOME PRECIOUS BEAUTY SLEEP.
LINC, ARE YOU OKAY? WHAT'S ALL THIS COMMOTION?
THEY'RE HERE, TOO!
SWOOSH
OH, HEY, LITTLE GUYS. THIS BIG WORLD MUST BE SCARY, HUH?
THEY'RE IN MY HAIR!
HUH?
LINCOLN, LINCOLN!

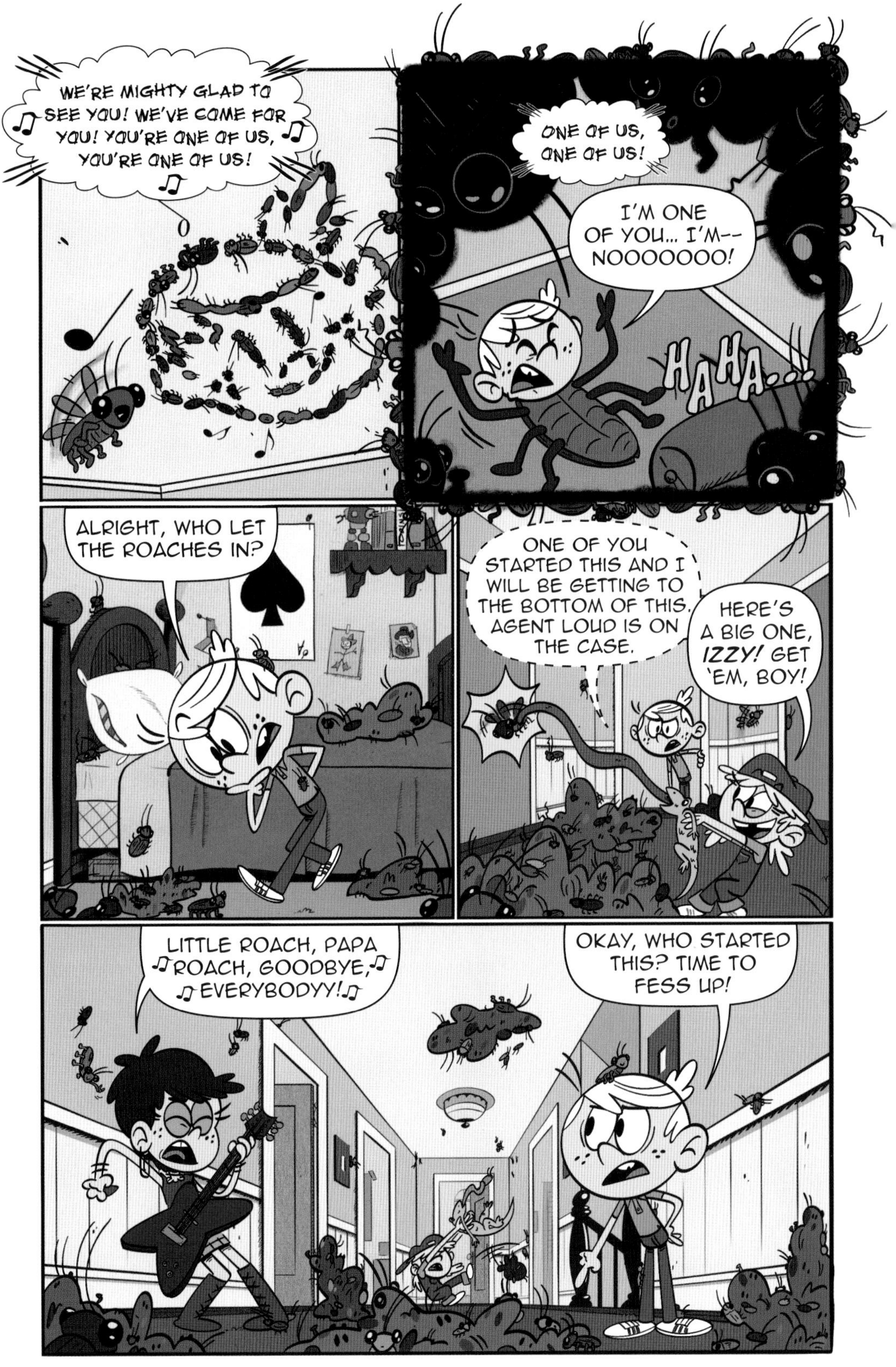

WE'RE MIGHTY GLAD TO SEE YOU! WE'VE COME FOR YOU! YOU'RE ONE OF US, YOU'RE ONE OF US!
ONE OF US, ONE OF US!
I'M ONE OF YOU... I'M-- NOOOOOOO!
HAHA...
ALRIGHT, WHO LET THE ROACHES IN?
ONE OF YOU STARTED THIS AND I WILL BE GETTING TO THE BOTTOM OF THIS. AGENT LOUD IS ON THE CASE.
HERE'S A BIG ONE, IZZY! GET 'EM, BOY!
LITTLE ROACH, PAPA ROACH, GOODBYE, EVERYBODYY!
OKAY, WHO STARTED THIS? TIME TO FESS UP!

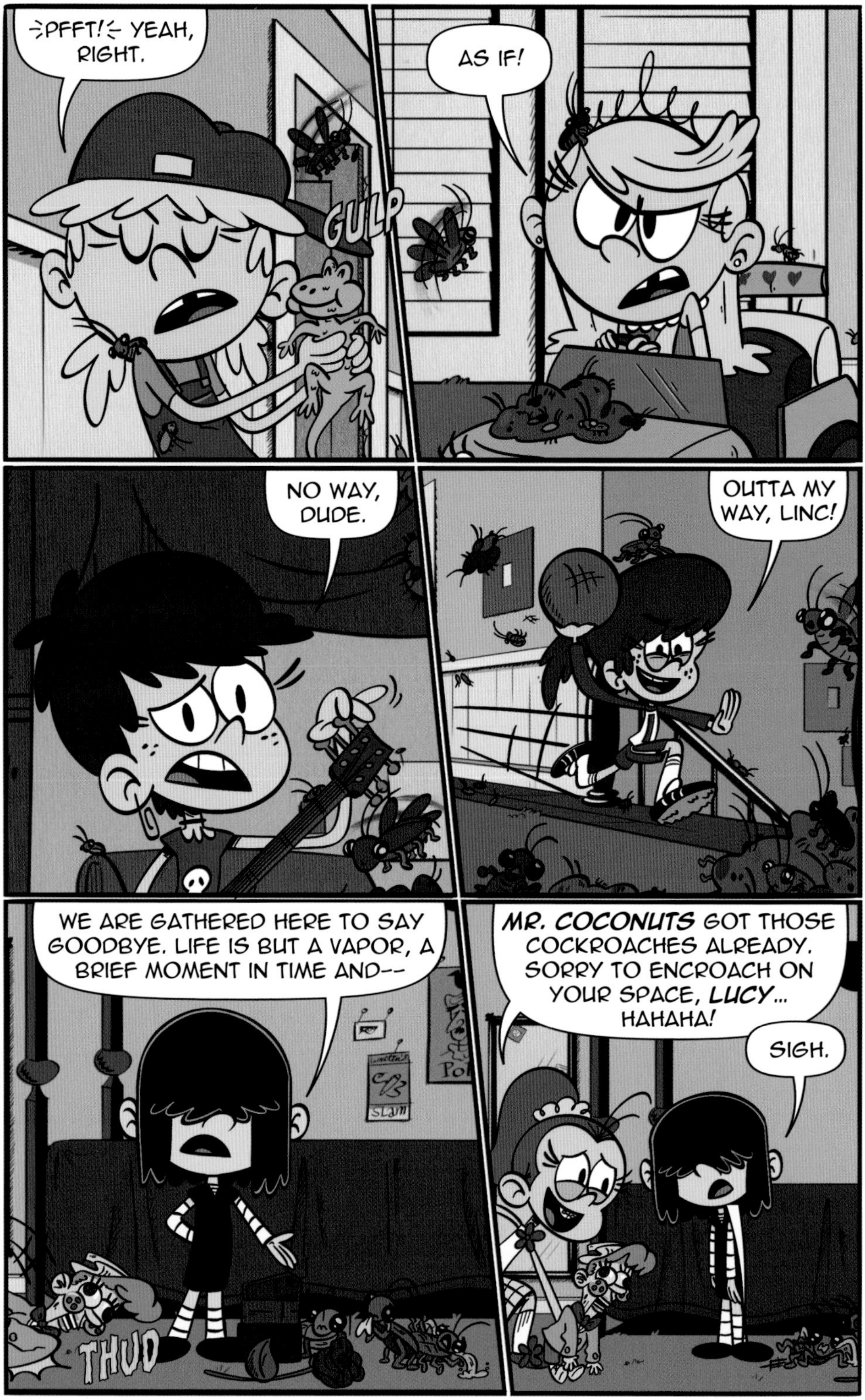
PFFT! YEAH, RIGHT.
GULP
AS IF!
NO WAY, DUDE.
OUTTA MY WAY, LINC!
WE ARE GATHERED HERE TO SAY GOODBYE. LIFE IS BUT A VAPOR, A BRIEF MOMENT IN TIME AND--
THUD
MR. COCONUTS GOT THOSE COCKROACHES ALREADY. SORRY TO ENCROACH ON YOUR SPACE, LUCY... HAHAHA!
SIGH.

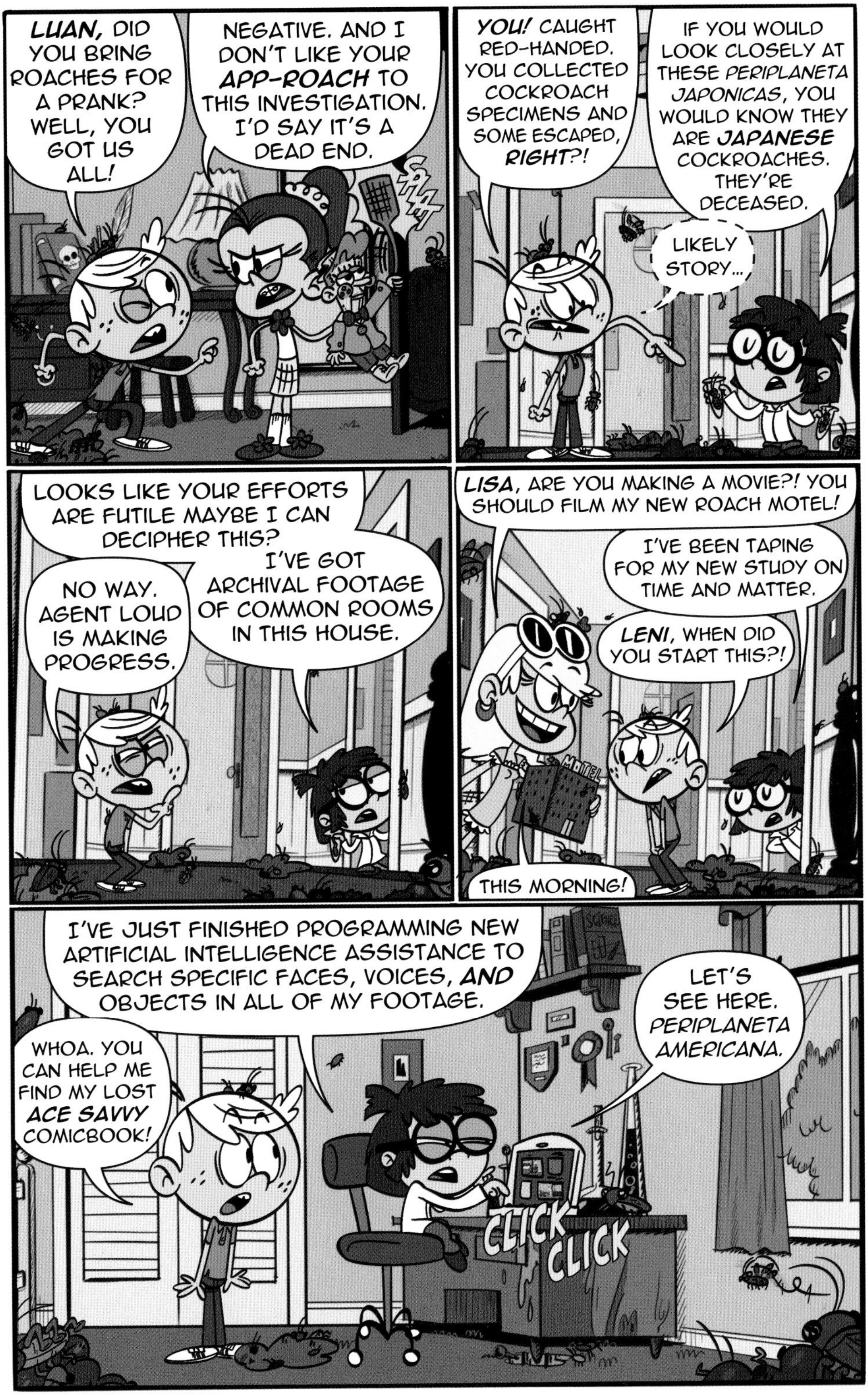
LUAN, DID YOU BRING ROACHES FOR A PRANK? WELL, YOU GOT US ALL!
NEGATIVE. AND I DON'T LIKE YOUR APP-ROACH TO THIS INVESTIGATION. I'D SAY IT'S A DEAD END.
YOU! CAUGHT RED-HANDED. YOU COLLECTED COCKROACH SPECIMENS AND SOME ESCAPED, RIGHT?!
IF YOU WOULD LOOK CLOSELY AT THESE PERIPLANETA JAPONICAS, YOU WOULD KNOW THEY ARE JAPANESE COCKROACHES. THEY'RE DECEASED.
LIKELY STORY...
LOOKS LIKE YOUR EFFORTS ARE FUTILE MAYBE I CAN DECIPHER THIS?
NO WAY. AGENT LOUD IS MAKING PROGRESS.
I'VE GOT ARCHIVAL FOOTAGE OF COMMON ROOMS IN THIS HOUSE.
LISA, ARE YOU MAKING A MOVIE?! YOU SHOULD FILM MY NEW ROACH MOTEL!
I'VE BEEN TAPING FOR MY NEW STUDY ON TIME AND MATTER.
LENI, WHEN DID YOU START THIS?!
THIS MORNING!
MOTEL
I'VE JUST FINISHED PROGRAMMING NEW ARTIFICIAL INTELLIGENCE ASSISTANCE TO SEARCH SPECIFIC FACES, VOICES, AND OBJECTS IN ALL OF MY FOOTAGE.
WHOA. YOU CAN HELP ME FIND MY LOST ACE SAVVY COMICBOOK!
LET'S SEE HERE. PERIPLANETA AMERICANA.
CLICK
CLICK

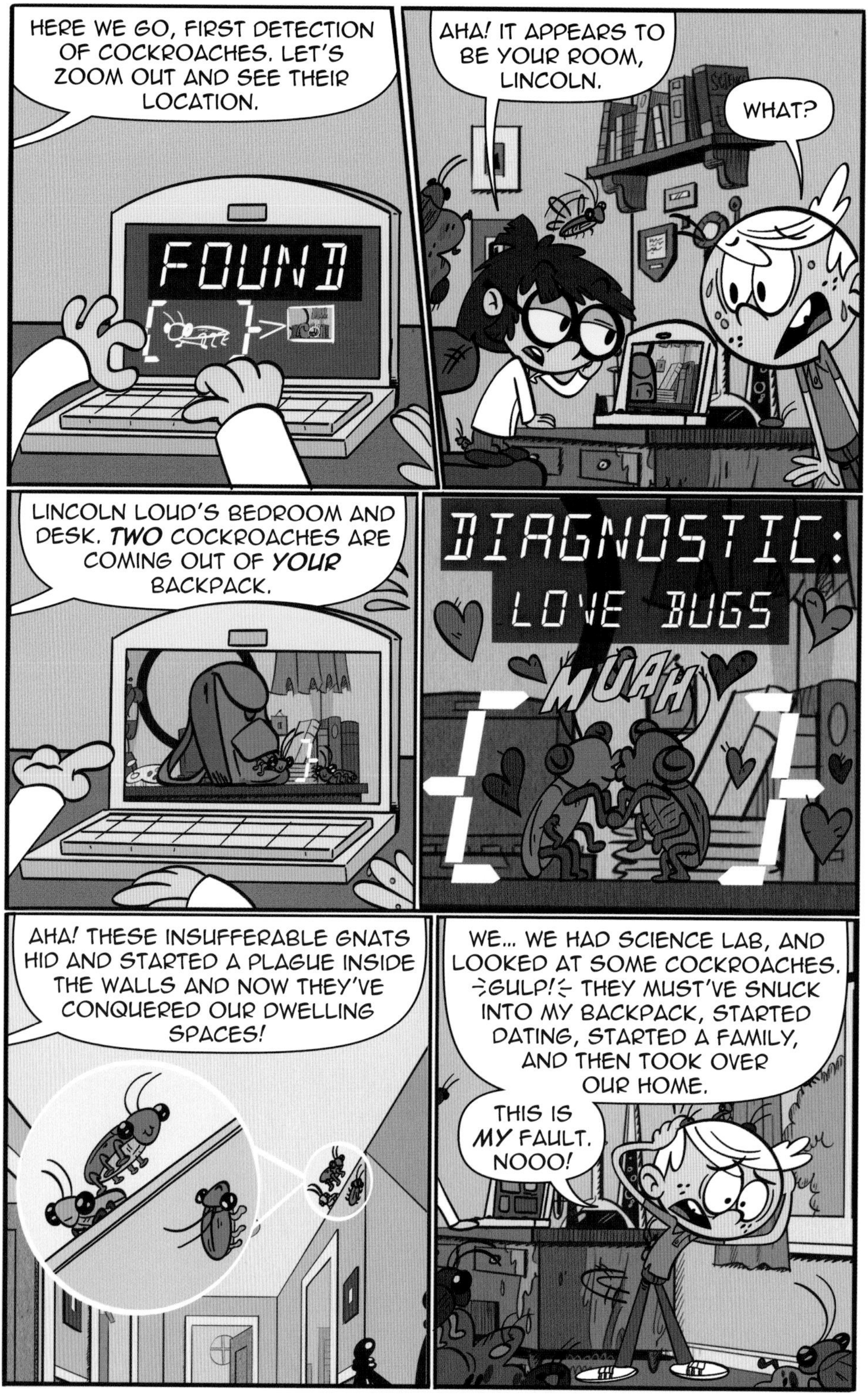
HERE WE GO, FIRST DETECTION OF COCKROACHES. LET'S ZOOM OUT AND SEE THEIR LOCATION.
FOUND
AHA! IT APPEARS TO BE YOUR ROOM, LINCOLN.
WHAT?
LINCOLN LOUD'S BEDROOM AND DESK. *TWO* COCKROACHES ARE COMING OUT OF *YOUR* BACKPACK.
DIAGNOSTIC:
LOVE BUGS
MUAH
AHA! THESE INSUFFERABLE GNATS HID AND STARTED A PLAGUE INSIDE THE WALLS AND NOW THEY'VE CONQUERED OUR DWELLING SPACES!
WE... WE HAD SCIENCE LAB, AND LOOKED AT SOME COCKROACHES. GULP! THEY MUST'VE SNUCK INTO MY BACKPACK, STARTED DATING, STARTED A FAMILY, AND THEN TOOK OVER OUR HOME.
THIS IS *MY* FAULT. NOOO!

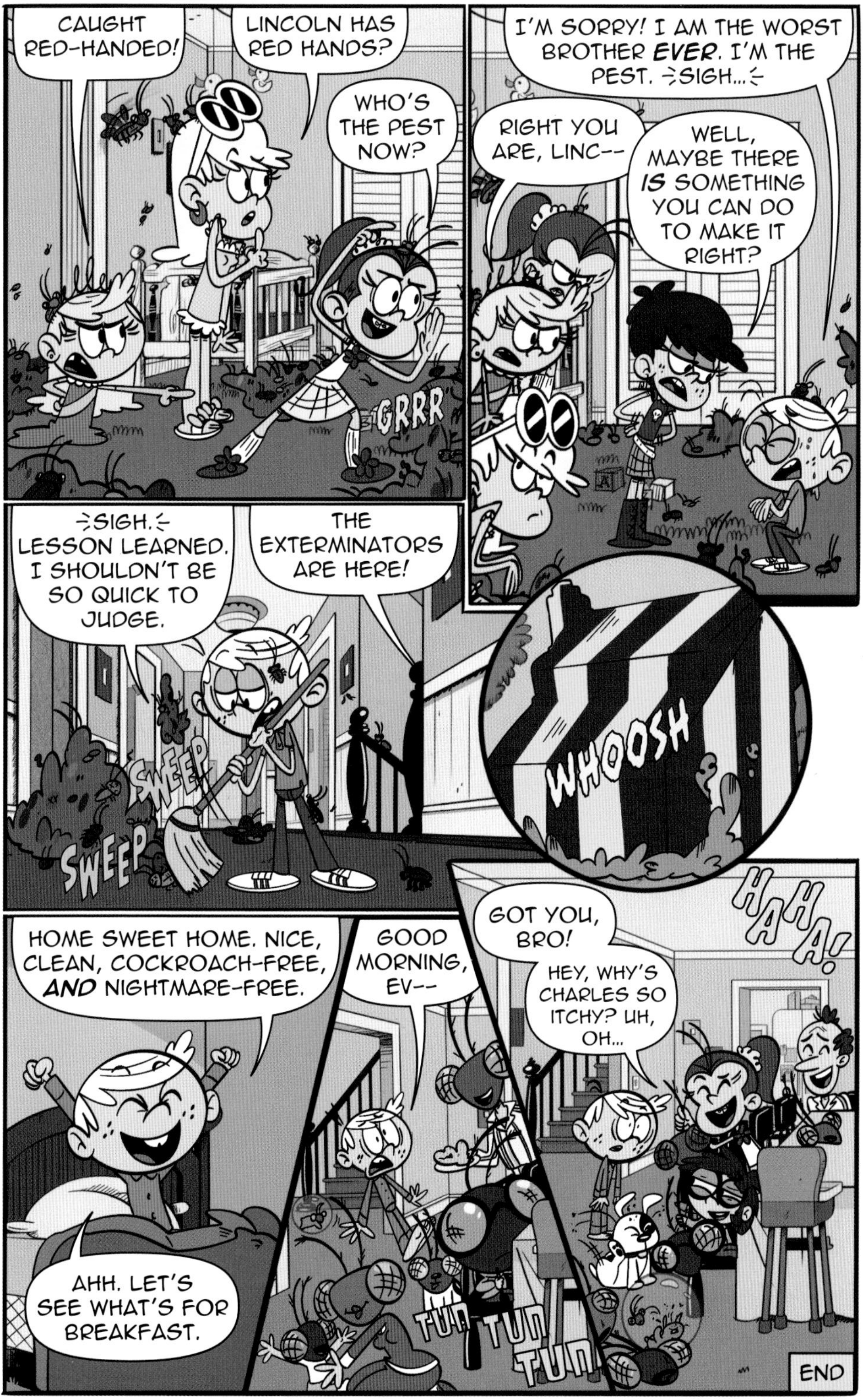
CAUGHT RED-HANDED!
LINCOLN HAS RED HANDS?
WHO'S THE PEST NOW?
GRRR
I'M SORRY! I AM THE WORST BROTHER *EVER*. I'M THE PEST. SIGH...
RIGHT YOU ARE, LINC--
WELL, MAYBE THERE *IS* SOMETHING YOU CAN DO TO MAKE IT RIGHT?
SIGH. LESSON LEARNED. I SHOULDN'T BE SO QUICK TO JUDGE.
THE EXTERMINATORS ARE HERE!
SWEEP
SWEEP
WHOOSH
HA HA HA!
HOME SWEET HOME. NICE, CLEAN, COCKROACH-FREE, *AND* NIGHTMARE-FREE.
AHH. LET'S SEE WHAT'S FOR BREAKFAST.
GOOD MORNING, EV--
TUN TUN TUN TUN
GOT YOU, BRO!
HEY, WHY'S CHARLES SO ITCHY? UH, OH...
END

“TH[illegible] NAM[illegible] CHA[illegible]L[illegible]. DO[illegible] CHA[illegible]L[illegible]”

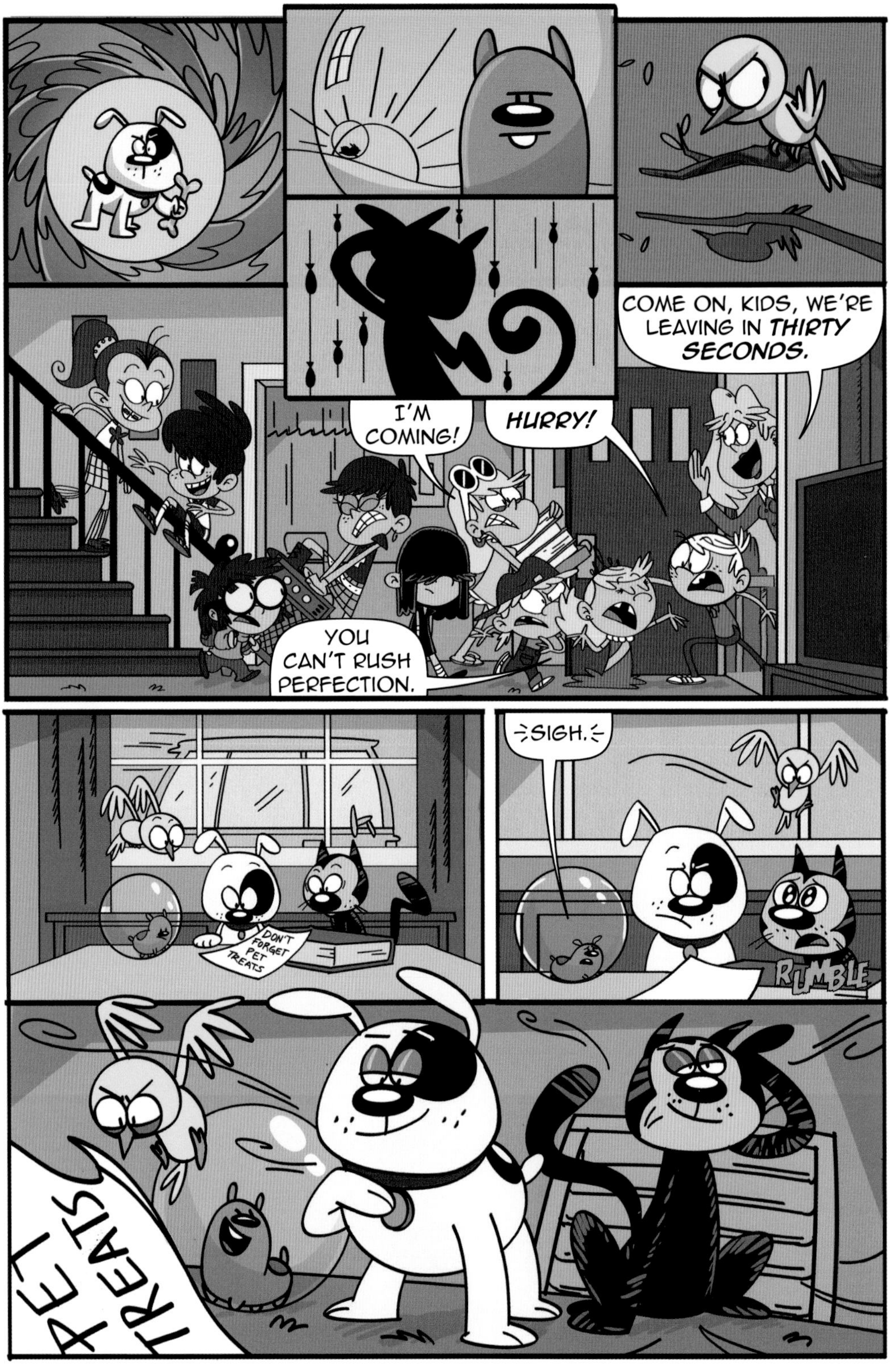

COME ON, KIDS, WE'RE LEAVING IN THIRTY SECONDS.
I'M COMING!
HURRY!
YOU CAN'T RUSH PERFECTION.
DON'T FORGET PET TREATS
SIGH.
RUMBLE
PET TREATS

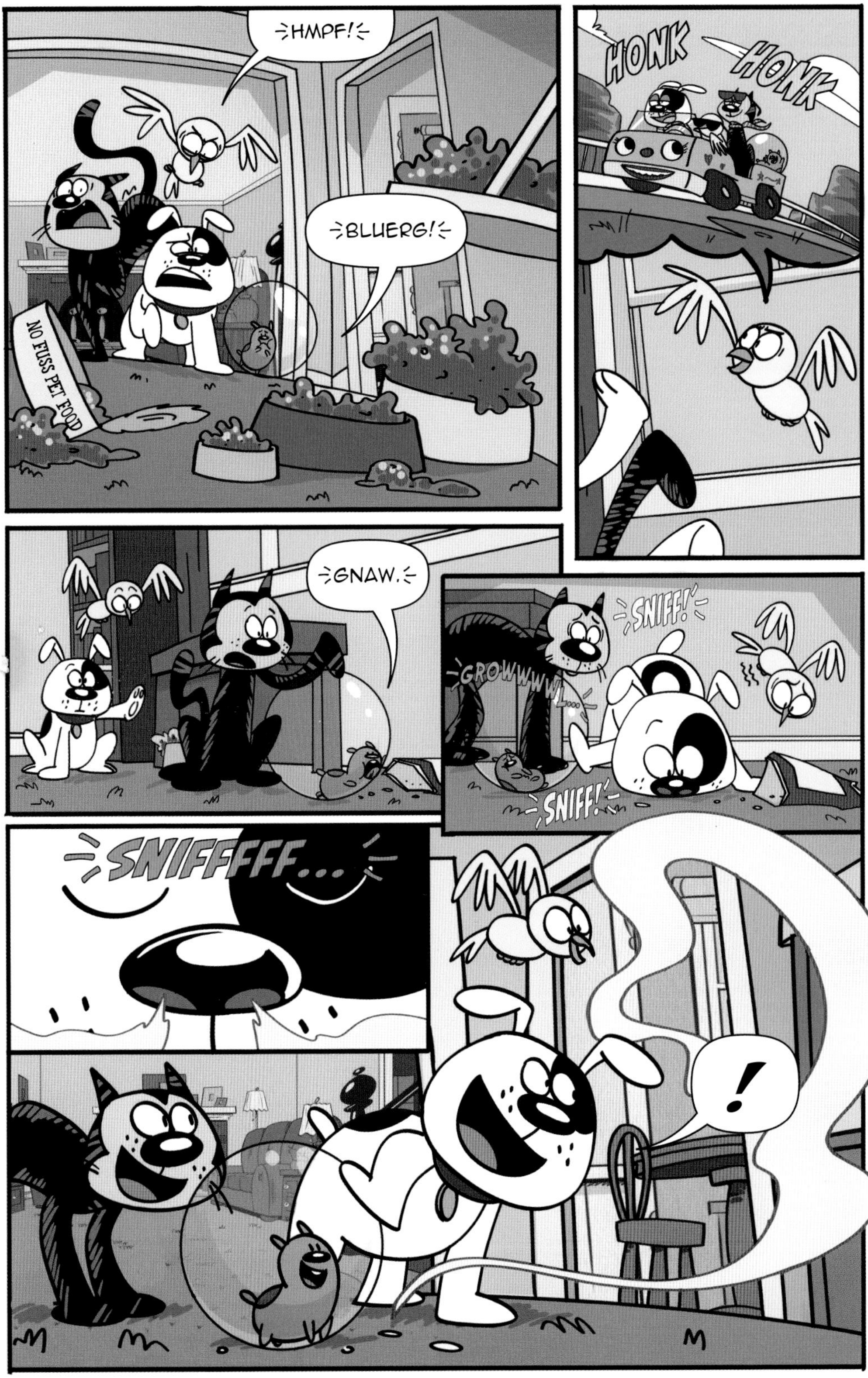
HMPF!
BLUERG!
NO FUSS PET FOOD
HONK
HONK
GNAW.
SNIFF!
GROWWWWL...
SNIFF!
SNIFFFFF...
!

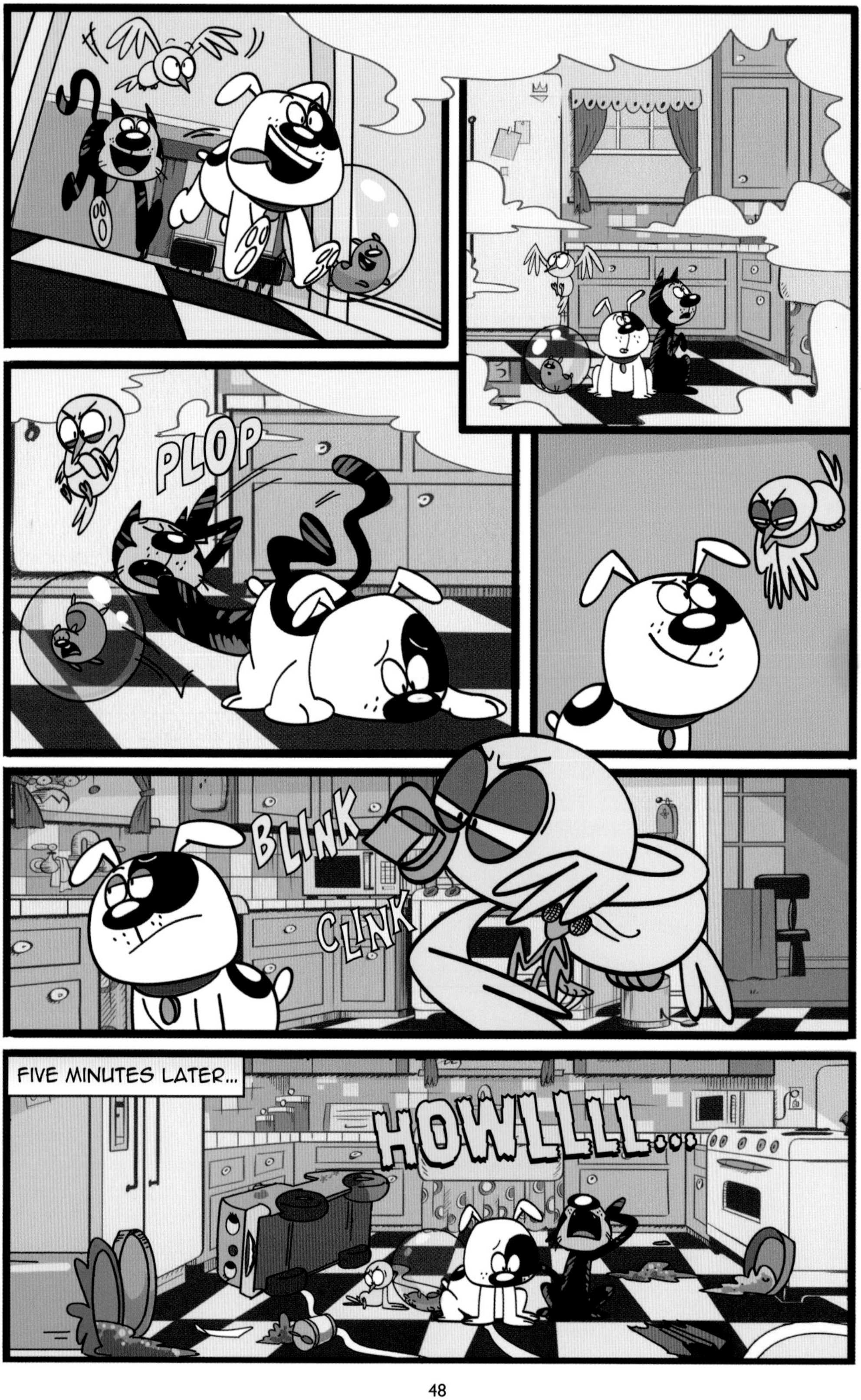
PLOP
BLINK
CLINK
FIVE MINUTES LATER...
HOWLLLL...

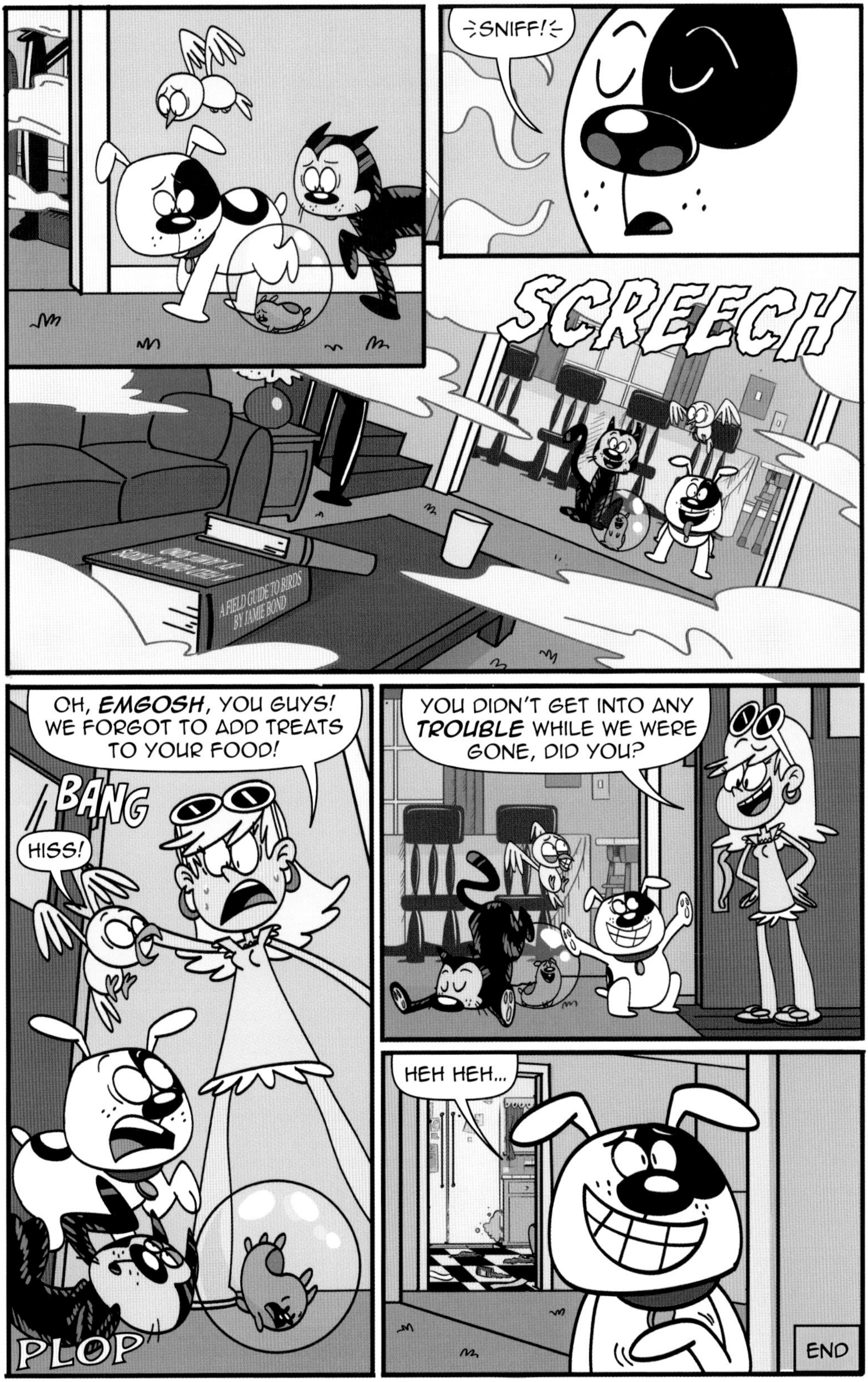

-SNIFF!-
SCREECH
A FIELD GUIDE TO BIRDS BY JAMIE BOND
OH, EMGOSH, YOU GUYS! WE FORGOT TO ADD TREATS TO YOUR FOOD!
BANG
HISS!
PLOP
YOU DIDN'T GET INTO ANY TROUBLE WHILE WE WERE GONE, DID YOU?
HEH HEH...
END

"BUBBLE TROUBLE"

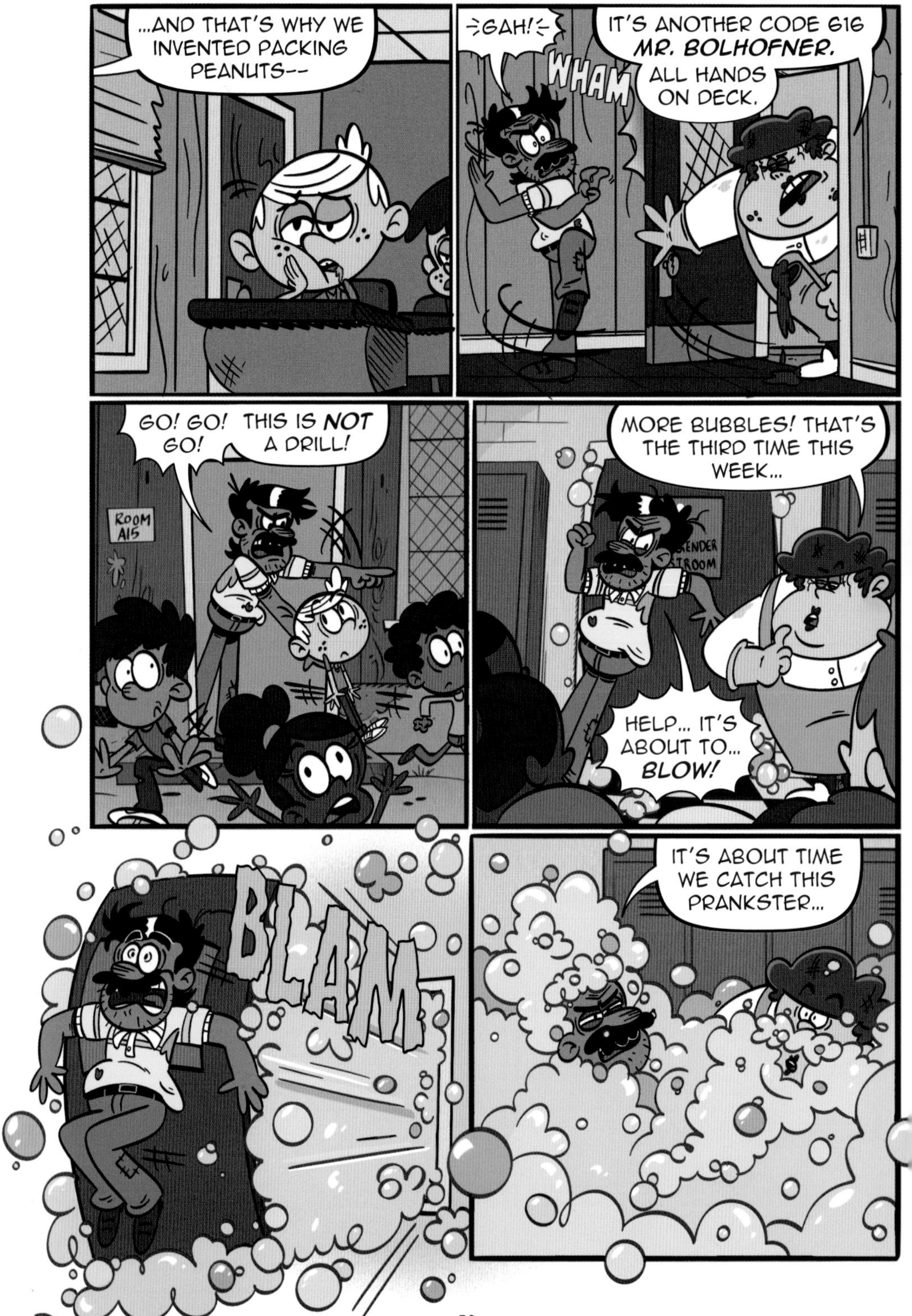

...AND THAT'S WHY WE INVENTED PACKING PEANUTS--
GAH!
WHAM
IT'S ANOTHER CODE 616 MR. BOLHOFNER.
ALL HANDS ON DECK.
GO! GO! GO!
THIS IS NOT A DRILL!
ROOM A15
MORE BUBBLES! THAT'S THE THIRD TIME THIS WEEK...
HELP... IT'S ABOUT TO... BLOW!
BLAM
IT'S ABOUT TIME WE CATCH THIS PRANKSTER...

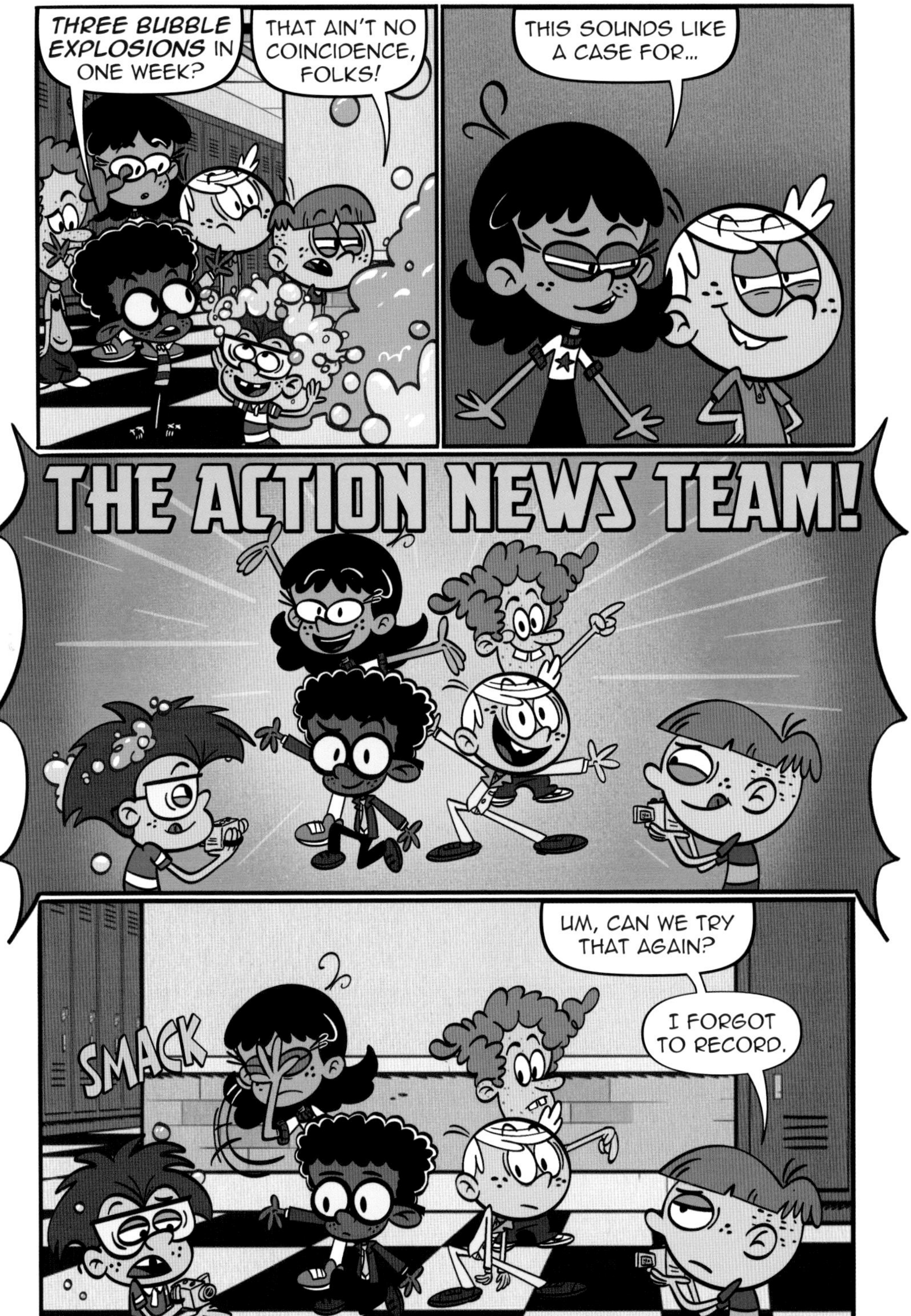
THREE BUBBLE EXPLOSIONS IN ONE WEEK?
THAT AIN'T NO COINCIDENCE, FOLKS!
THIS SOUNDS LIKE A CASE FOR...
THE ACTION NEWS TEAM!
UM, CAN WE TRY THAT AGAIN?
I FORGOT TO RECORD.
SMACK

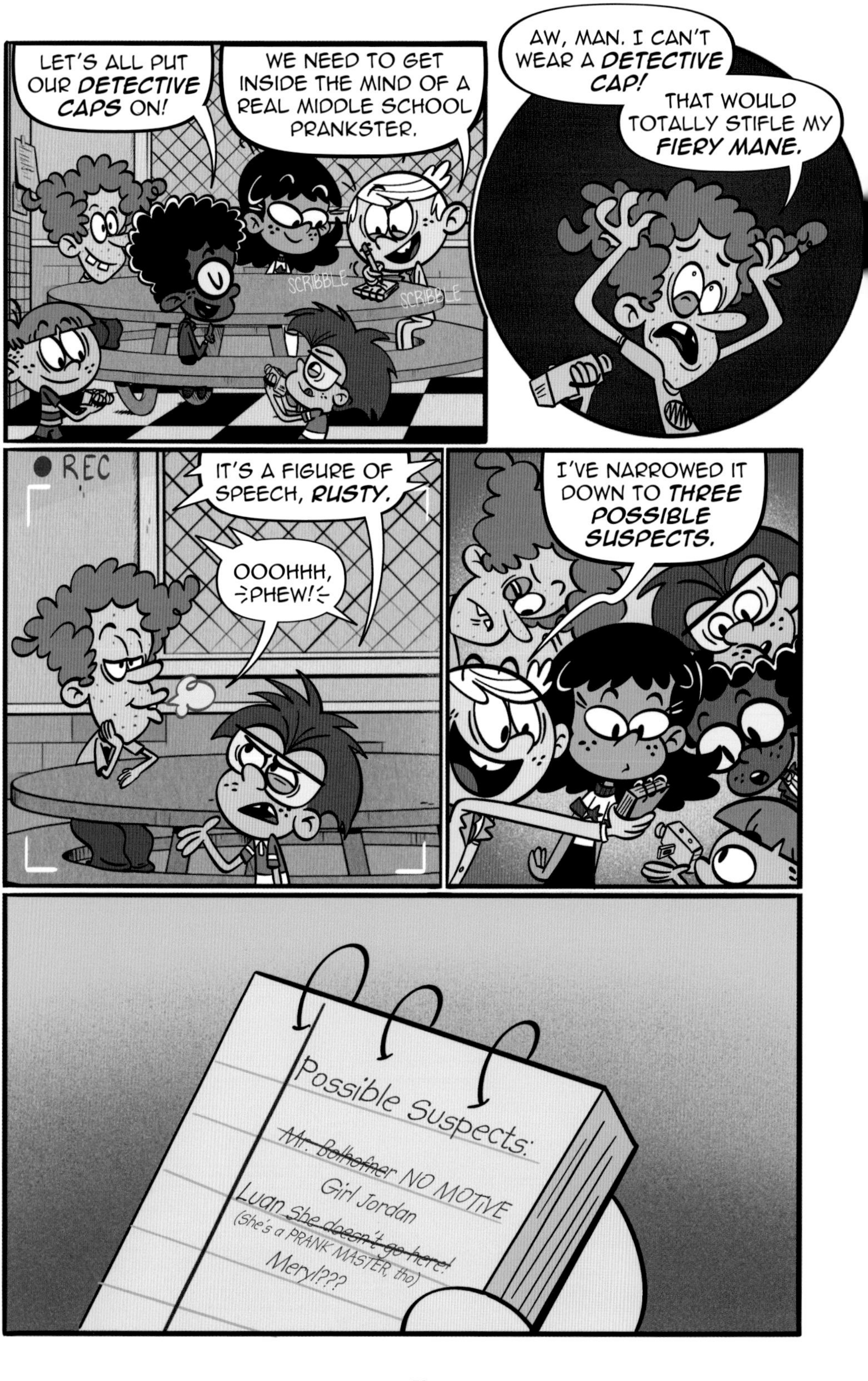
LET'S ALL PUT OUR DETECTIVE CAPS ON!
WE NEED TO GET INSIDE THE MIND OF A REAL MIDDLE SCHOOL PRANKSTER.
SCRIBBLE
SCRIBBLE
AW, MAN. I CAN'T WEAR A DETECTIVE CAP!
THAT WOULD TOTALLY STIFLE MY FIERY MANE.
REC
IT'S A FIGURE OF SPEECH, RUSTY.
OOOHHH, PHEW!
I'VE NARROWED IT DOWN TO THREE POSSIBLE SUSPECTS.
Possible Suspects:
~~Mr. Bolhofner~~ NO MOTIVE
Girl Jordan
Luan ~~She doesn't go here!~~
(She's a PRANK MASTER, tho)
Meryl???

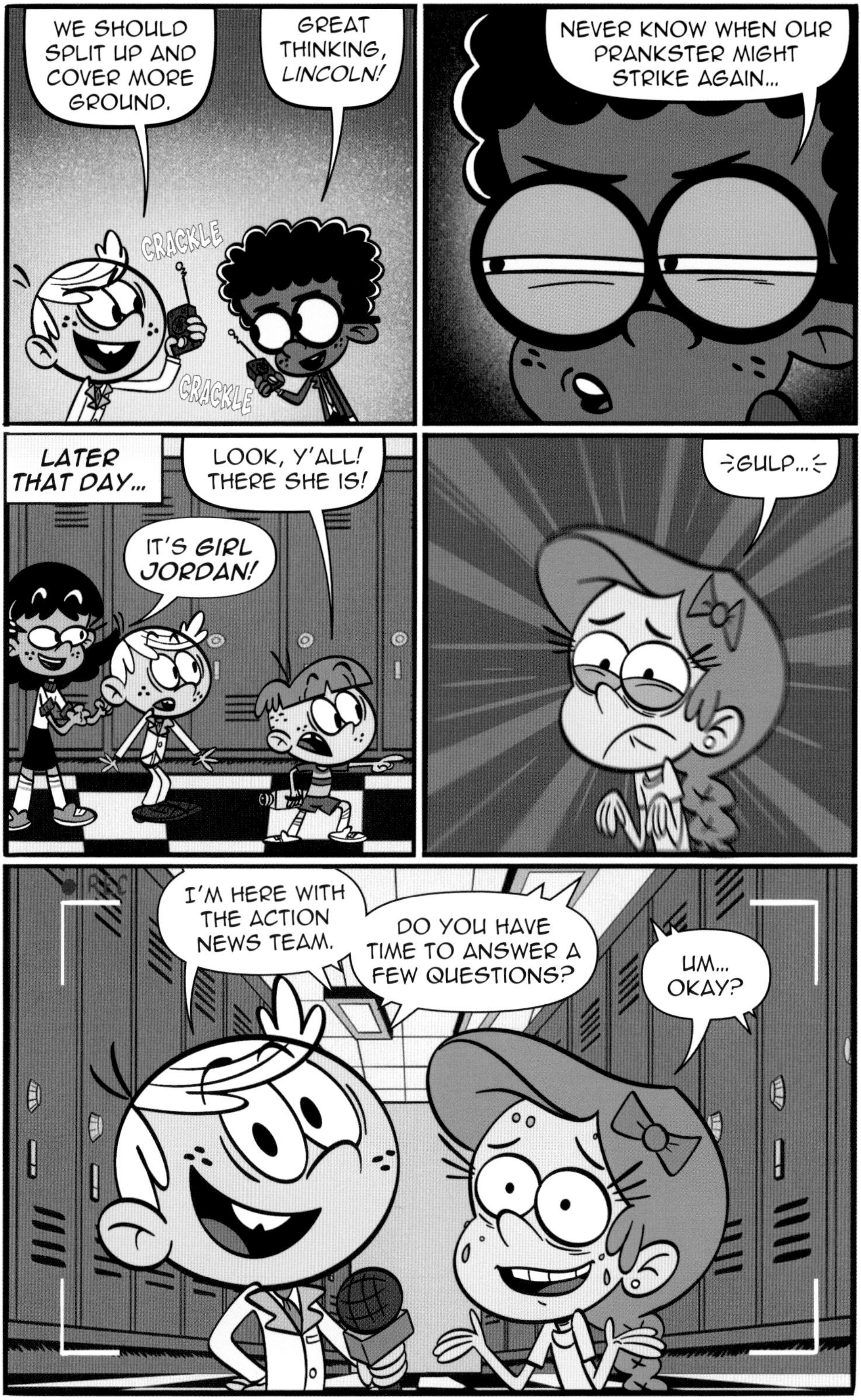
WE SHOULD SPLIT UP AND COVER MORE GROUND.
GREAT THINKING, LINCOLN!
CRACKLE
CRACKLE
NEVER KNOW WHEN OUR PRANKSTER MIGHT STRIKE AGAIN...
LATER THAT DAY...
LOOK, Y'ALL! THERE SHE IS!
IT'S GIRL JORDAN!
GULP...
I'M HERE WITH THE ACTION NEWS TEAM.
DO YOU HAVE TIME TO ANSWER A FEW QUESTIONS?
UM... OKAY?

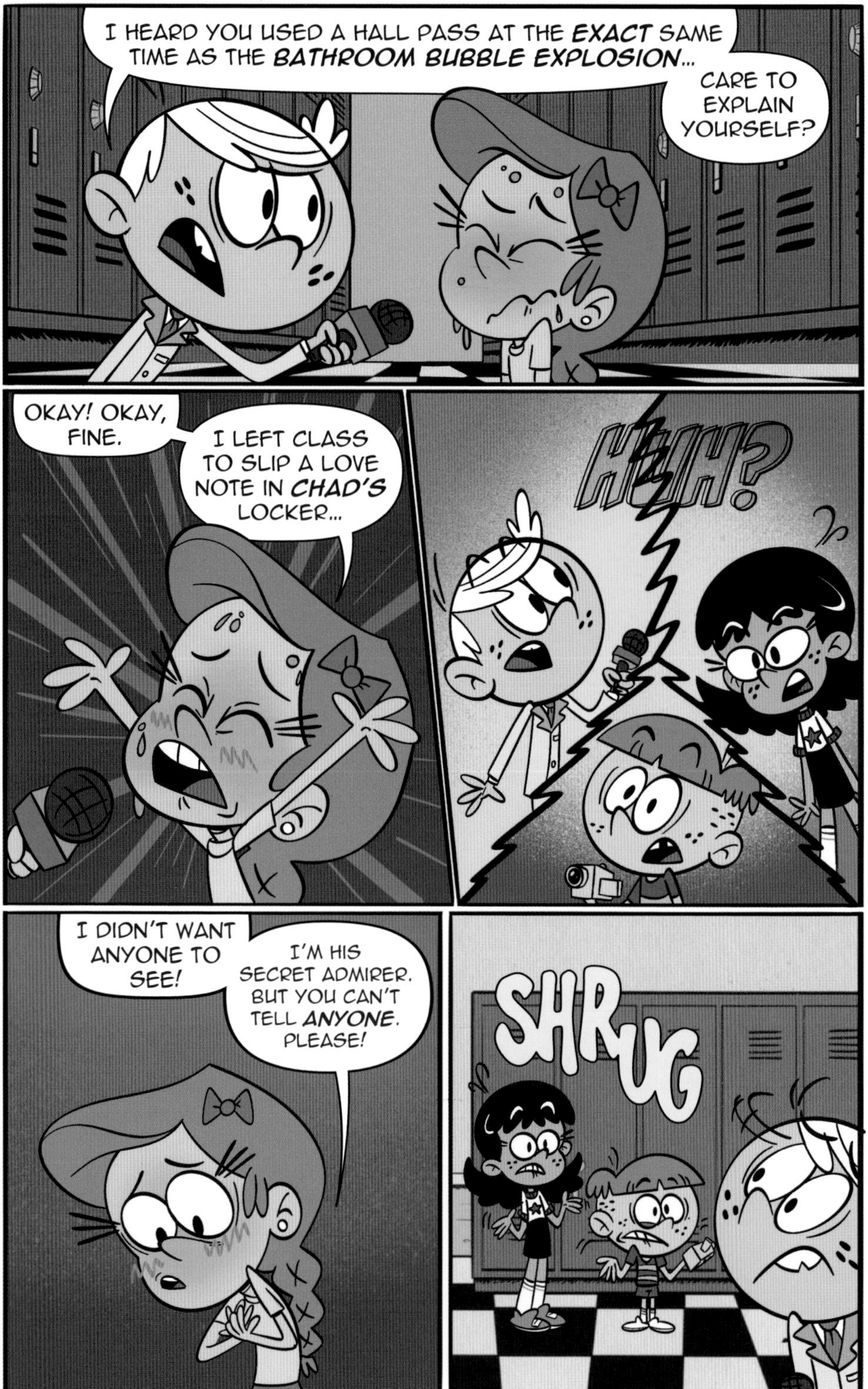
I HEARD YOU USED A HALL PASS AT THE EXACT SAME TIME AS THE BATHROOM BUBBLE EXPLOSION...
CARE TO EXPLAIN YOURSELF?
OKAY! OKAY, FINE.
I LEFT CLASS TO SLIP A LOVE NOTE IN CHAD'S LOCKER...
HUH?
I DIDN'T WANT ANYONE TO SEE!
I'M HIS SECRET ADMIRER. BUT YOU CAN'T TELL ANYONE. PLEASE!
SHRUG

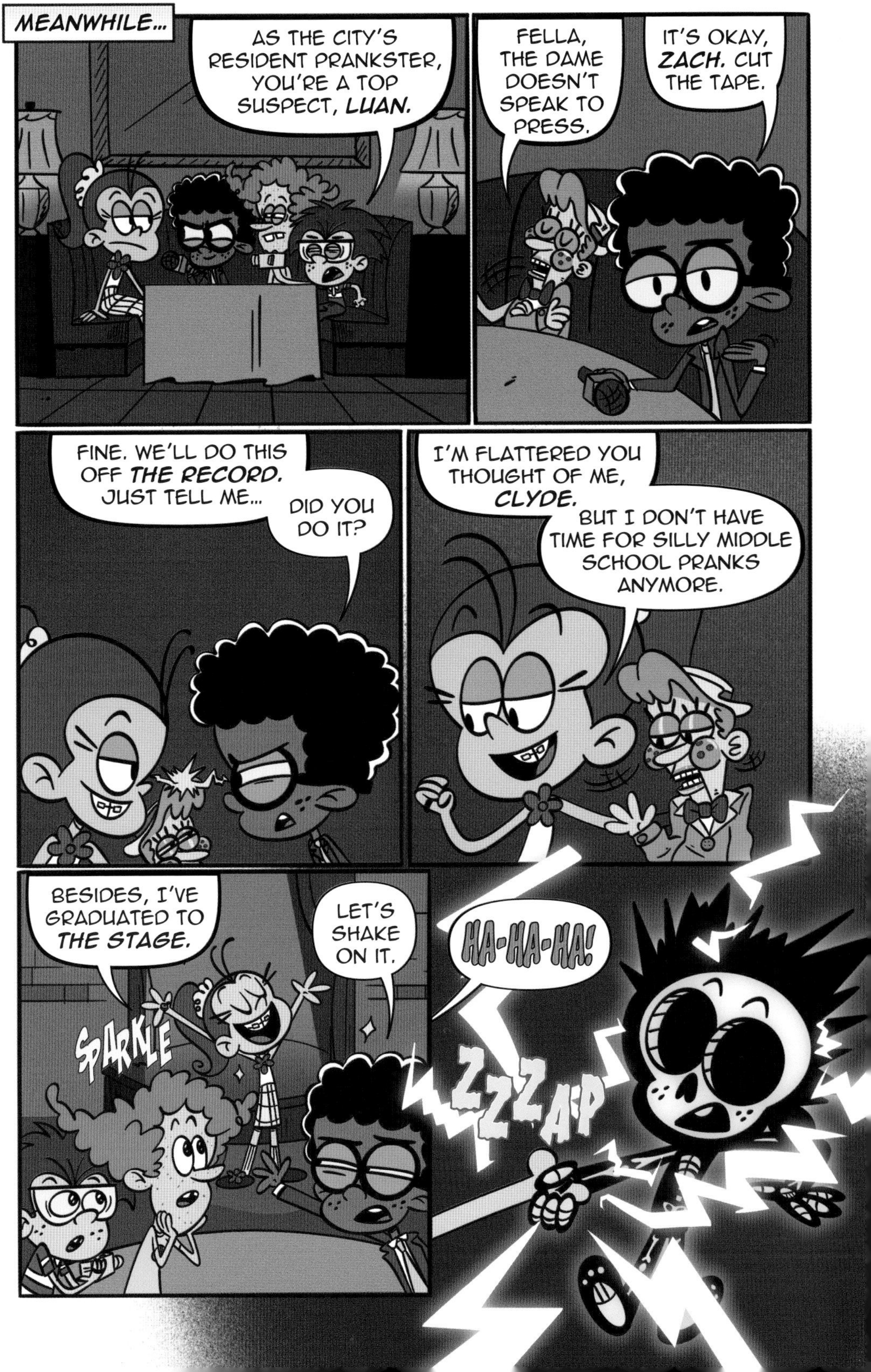
MEANWHILE...
AS THE CITY'S RESIDENT PRANKSTER, YOU'RE A TOP SUSPECT, LUAN.
FELLA, THE DAME DOESN'T SPEAK TO PRESS.
IT'S OKAY, ZACH. CUT THE TAPE.
FINE. WE'LL DO THIS OFF THE RECORD. JUST TELL ME...
DID YOU DO IT?
I'M FLATTERED YOU THOUGHT OF ME, CLYDE.
BUT I DON'T HAVE TIME FOR SILLY MIDDLE SCHOOL PRANKS ANYMORE.
BESIDES, I'VE GRADUATED TO THE STAGE.
LET'S SHAKE ON IT.
SPARKLE
HA-HA-HA!
ZZZAP

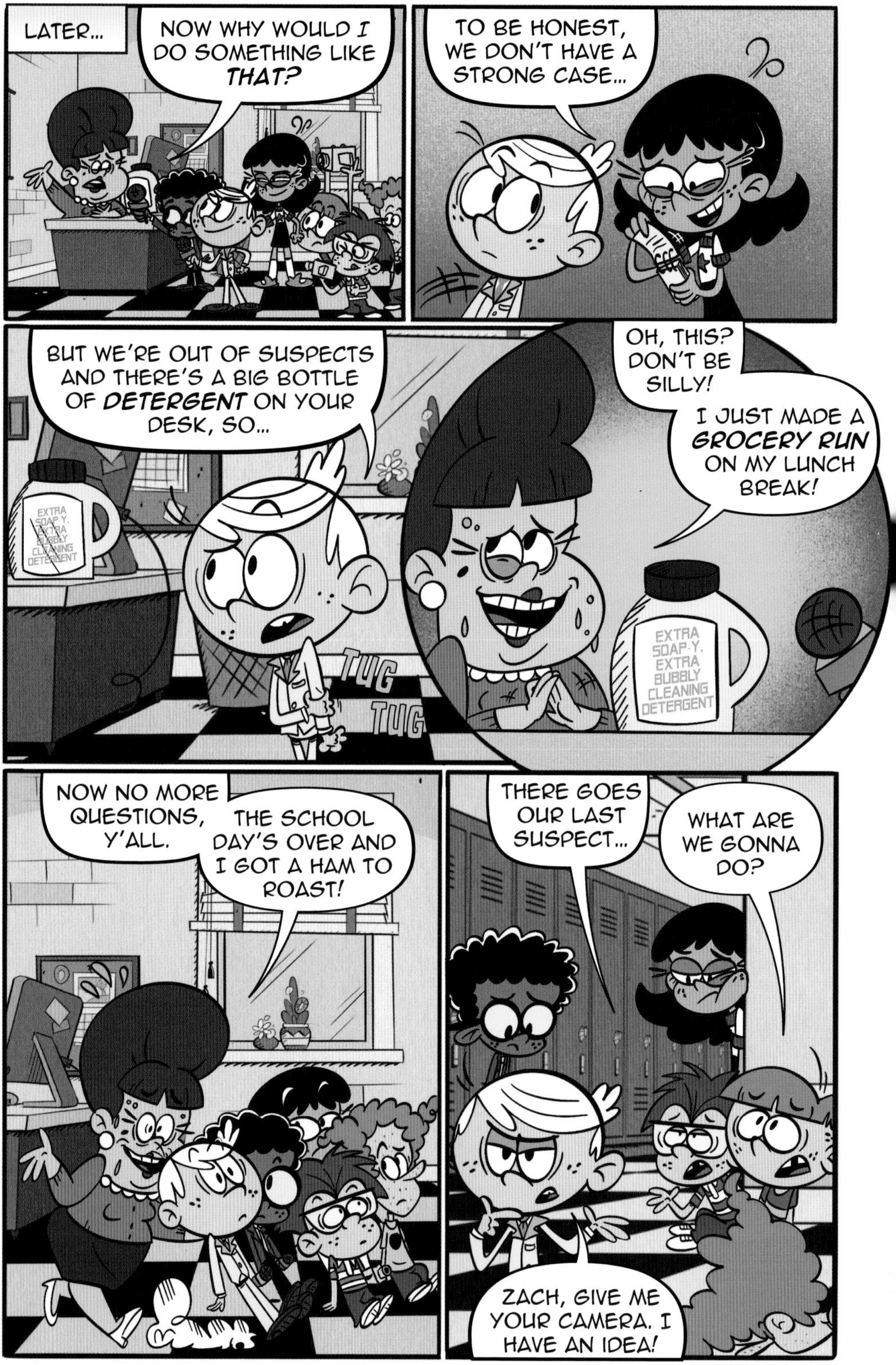
LATER...
NOW WHY WOULD I DO SOMETHING LIKE THAT?
TO BE HONEST, WE DON'T HAVE A STRONG CASE...
BUT WE'RE OUT OF SUSPECTS AND THERE'S A BIG BOTTLE OF DETERGENT ON YOUR DESK, SO...
EXTRA SOAP-Y, EXTRA BUBBLY CLEANING DETERGENT
TUG TUG
OH, THIS? DON'T BE SILLY!
I JUST MADE A GROCERY RUN ON MY LUNCH BREAK!
EXTRA SOAP-Y, EXTRA BUBBLY CLEANING DETERGENT
NOW NO MORE QUESTIONS, Y'ALL.
THE SCHOOL DAY'S OVER AND I GOT A HAM TO ROAST!
THERE GOES OUR LAST SUSPECT...
WHAT ARE WE GONNA DO?
ZACH, GIVE ME YOUR CAMERA. I HAVE AN IDEA!

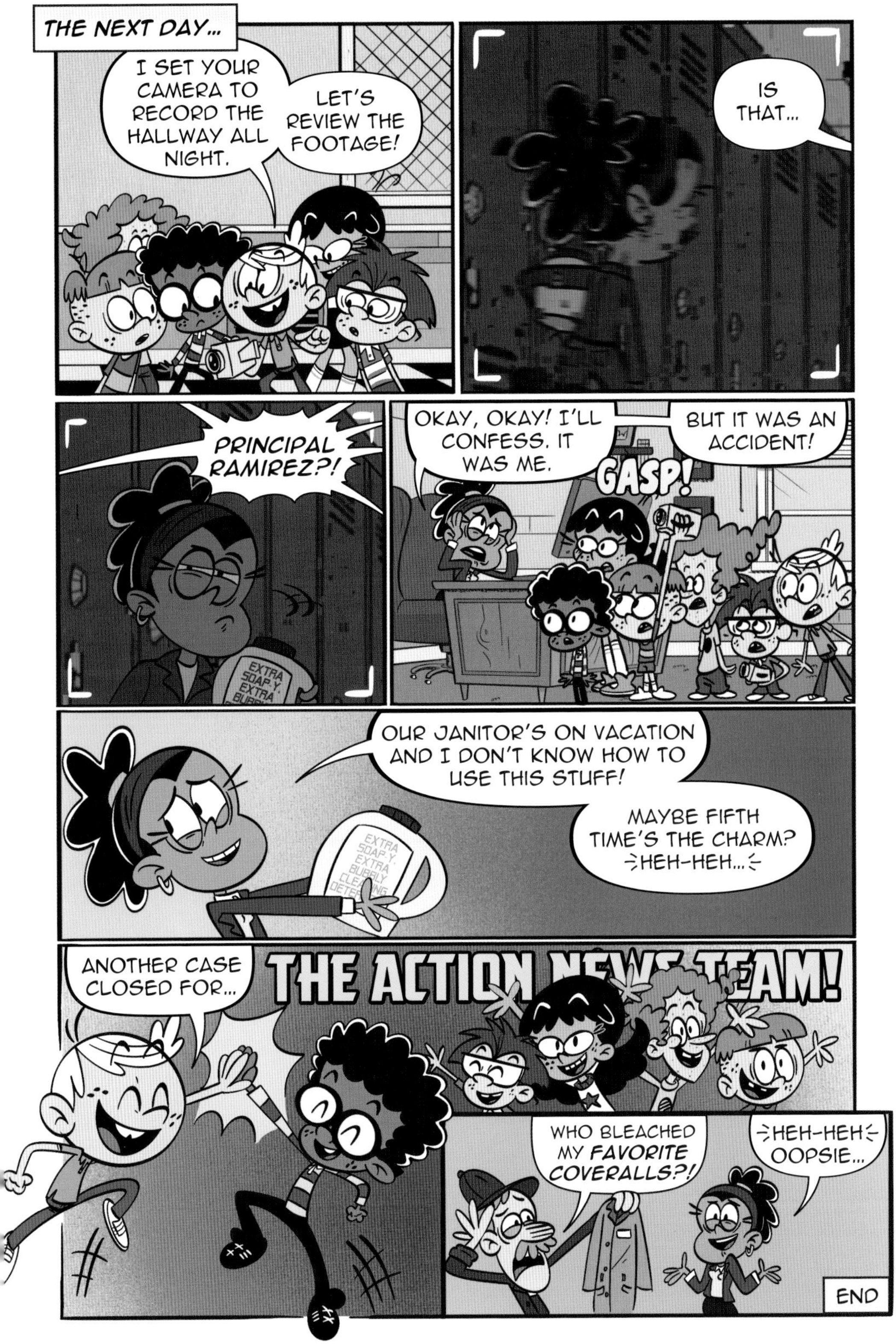
THE NEXT DAY...
I SET YOUR CAMERA TO RECORD THE HALLWAY ALL NIGHT.
LET'S REVIEW THE FOOTAGE!
IS THAT...
PRINCIPAL RAMIREZ?!
EXTRA SOAP-Y EXTRA BUBBLY
OKAY, OKAY! I'LL CONFESS. IT WAS ME.
BUT IT WAS AN ACCIDENT!
GASP!
OUR JANITOR'S ON VACATION AND I DON'T KNOW HOW TO USE THIS STUFF!
MAYBE FIFTH TIME'S THE CHARM? HEH-HEH...
EXTRA SOAP-Y EXTRA BUBBLY CLEANING DETERGENT
ANOTHER CASE CLOSED FOR...
THE ACTION NEWS TEAM!
WHO BLEACHED MY FAVORITE COVERALLS?!
HEH-HEH OOPSIE...
END

THE GADGETRY OF AGENT DAVID STEELE

REPORT BY
JUNIOR AGENT
LINCOLN LOUD

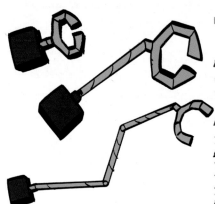

THE STEELE CLAW

FIRST APPEARANCE:

VOLUME 2, ISSUE 23
"STEELE OR NO STEELE"

NOTES:

THE PERFECT TOOL FOR STEALTHY
EXTRACTION... AS LONG AS IT'S WITHIN
THREE FEET OF YOU. OH! I COULD USE IT
TO STEAL TOP SECRET FILES FROM GOLDEN
TOE! OR JUST TAKE THE REMOTE BACK
FROM LANA ON THE COUCH. BOTH WORK.

SPY-NOCULARS

FIRST APPEARANCE:

VOLUME 3, ISSUE 8
"FOR YOUR EYES, TONY"

NOTES:

DAVID STEELE'S SPY-NOCULARS CAN
SPOT BLOW FISH'S MOON LAIR ALL THE
WAY FROM EARTH! MINE CAN ONLY SEE
WHAT MR. GROUSE IS UP TO FROM
MY WINDOW. IT'S USUALLY NAPPING.
NOTE TO SELF: SEND SPY-NOCULARS
TO LISA FOR LUNAR UPGRADE.

THE LIQUID LAUNCHER

FIRST APPEARANCE:

VOLUME 6, ISSUE 100
"LIVE AND LIQUID"

NOTES:

YOU KNOW THE OLD SAYING. IF IT'S
A LIQUID, IT CAN BE BLASTED! FOR
MAXIMUM SPLATTAGE, I FOUND THE
BEST RESULTS WITH DAD'S RED
LYNN-GUINI SAUCE. MEATBALLS ARE
OPTIONAL. I WONDER IF I CAN FILL
IT WITH A FLIPPEE... WILL RETURN
WITH RESULTS!

THE FLASHLIGHT WATCH

FIRST APPEARANCE:

VOLUME 2, ISSUE 35
"TOMORROW NEVER SHINES"

NOTES:

WITHOUT THIS WATCH, DAVID STEELE AND I WOULD STILL BE LEFT IN THE DARK! OF COURSE, HE WAS LOST UNDER M.A.L.I.C.E.'S VOLCANO BASE, AND I WAS STUCK GETTING MY LAUNDRY FROM OUR DARK BASEMENT, BUT YOU GET THE IDEA.

DAVID STEELE
DAVID STEELE

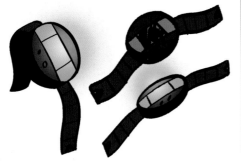

"AGENT D. RONE" (AND CONTROLLER)

FIRST APPEARANCE:

VOLUME 1, ISSUE 16
"LET'S MAKE A STEELE"

NOTES:

TARGET'S ON THE MOVE? NO PROBLEM FOR YOUR SPY IN THE SKY! WOULD NOT RECOMMEND FLYING INDOORS THOUGH. ACCIDENTALLY TOOK OFF FLIP'S MUSTACHE WITH THE PROPELLERS. IT'S GROWING BACK NICELY THOUGH!

THE WALKIE TALKIE

FIRST APPEARANCE:

VOLUME 2, ISSUE 1
"ALLOY'S ALLY"

NOTES:

YOU WALKIE TALKIN' TO ME? NO AGENT IS COMPLETE WITHOUT ONE! HOW ELSE ARE YOU SUPPOSED TO TELL YOUR FELLOW AGENT THAT YOUR NEIGHBORS ARE SPIES, BUT YOUR FAMILY DOESN'T BELIEVE YOU, SO YOU HAVE TO GATHER EVIDENCE?

Check out a preview of THE CASAGRANDES #6!

"THE INTERNSHIP"

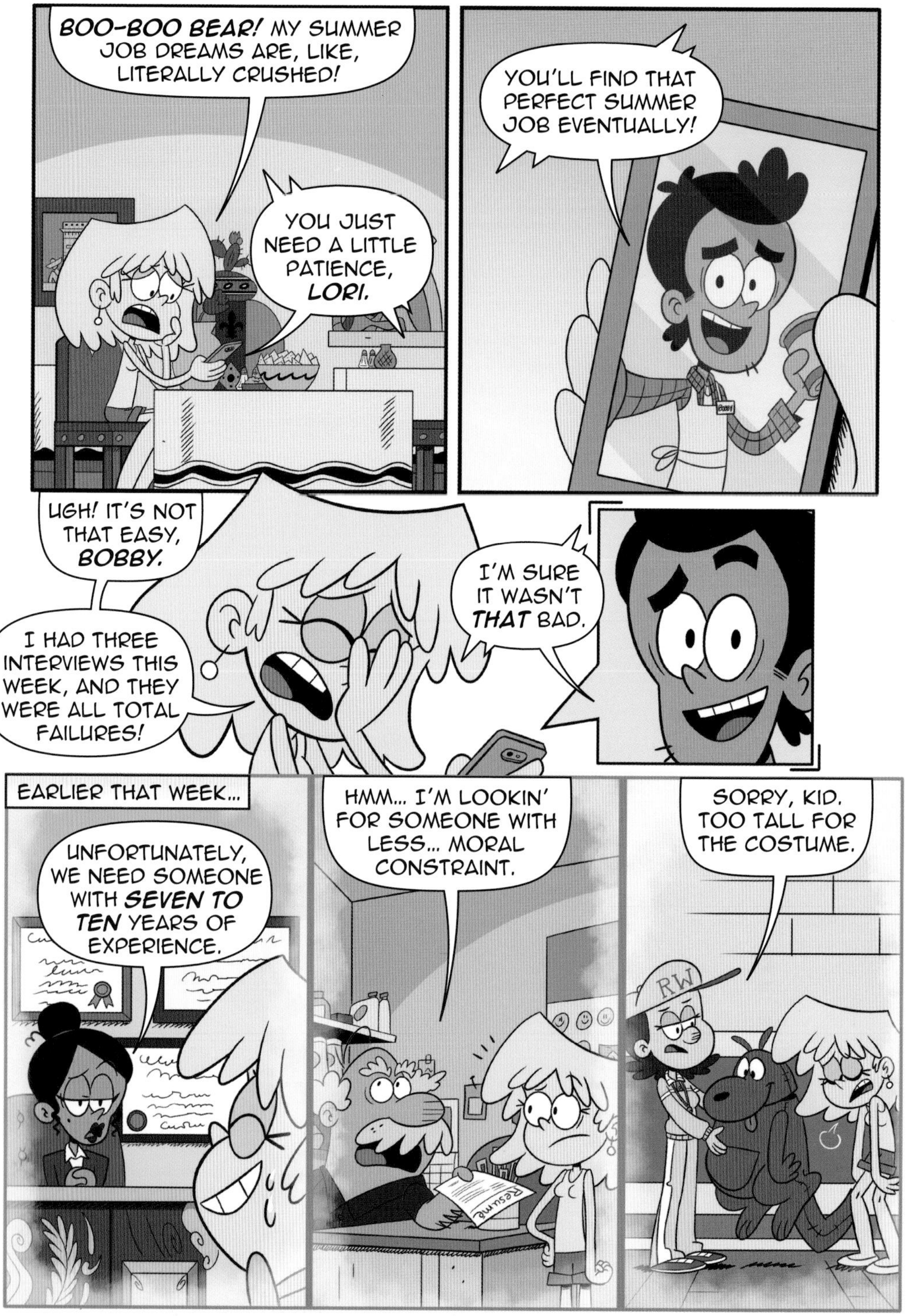
BOO-BOO BEAR! MY SUMMER JOB DREAMS ARE, LIKE, LITERALLY CRUSHED!
YOU JUST NEED A LITTLE PATIENCE, LORI.
YOU'LL FIND THAT PERFECT SUMMER JOB EVENTUALLY!
UGH! IT'S NOT THAT EASY, BOBBY.
I HAD THREE INTERVIEWS THIS WEEK, AND THEY WERE ALL TOTAL FAILURES!
I'M SURE IT WASN'T THAT BAD.
EARLIER THAT WEEK...
UNFORTUNATELY, WE NEED SOMEONE WITH SEVEN TO TEN YEARS OF EXPERIENCE.
HMM... I'M LOOKIN' FOR SOMEONE WITH LESS... MORAL CONSTRAINT.
Resume
SORRY, KID. TOO TALL FOR THE COSTUME.
RW

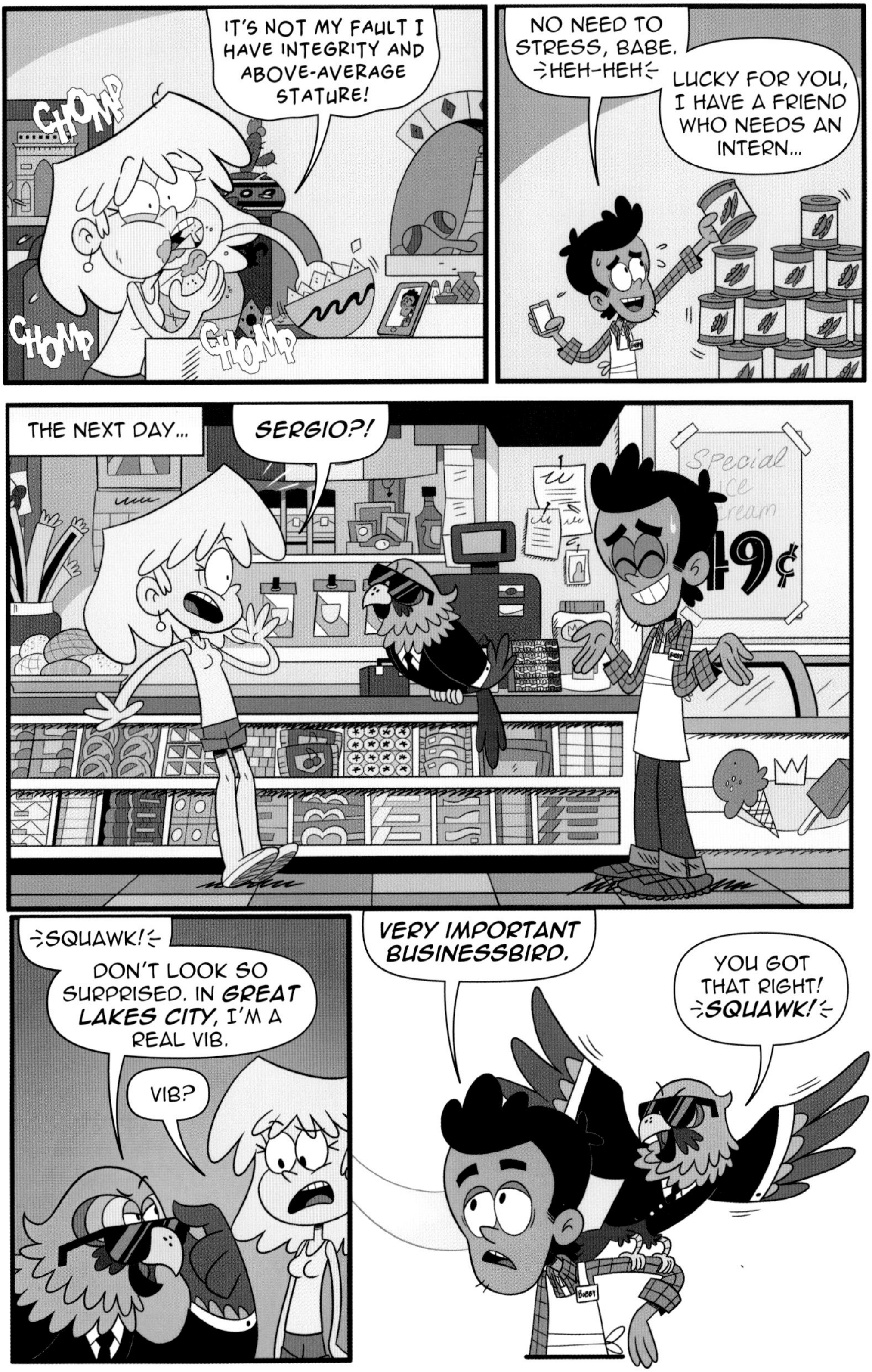

IT'S NOT MY FAULT I HAVE INTEGRITY AND ABOVE-AVERAGE STATURE!
CHOMP
CHOMP
CHOMP
NO NEED TO STRESS, BABE. HEH-HEH
LUCKY FOR YOU, I HAVE A FRIEND WHO NEEDS AN INTERN...
THE NEXT DAY...
SERGIO?!
Special Ice Cream
49¢
SQUAWK!
DON'T LOOK SO SURPRISED. IN GREAT LAKES CITY, I'M A REAL VIB.
VIB?
VERY IMPORTANT BUSINESSBIRD.
YOU GOT THAT RIGHT! SQUAWK!

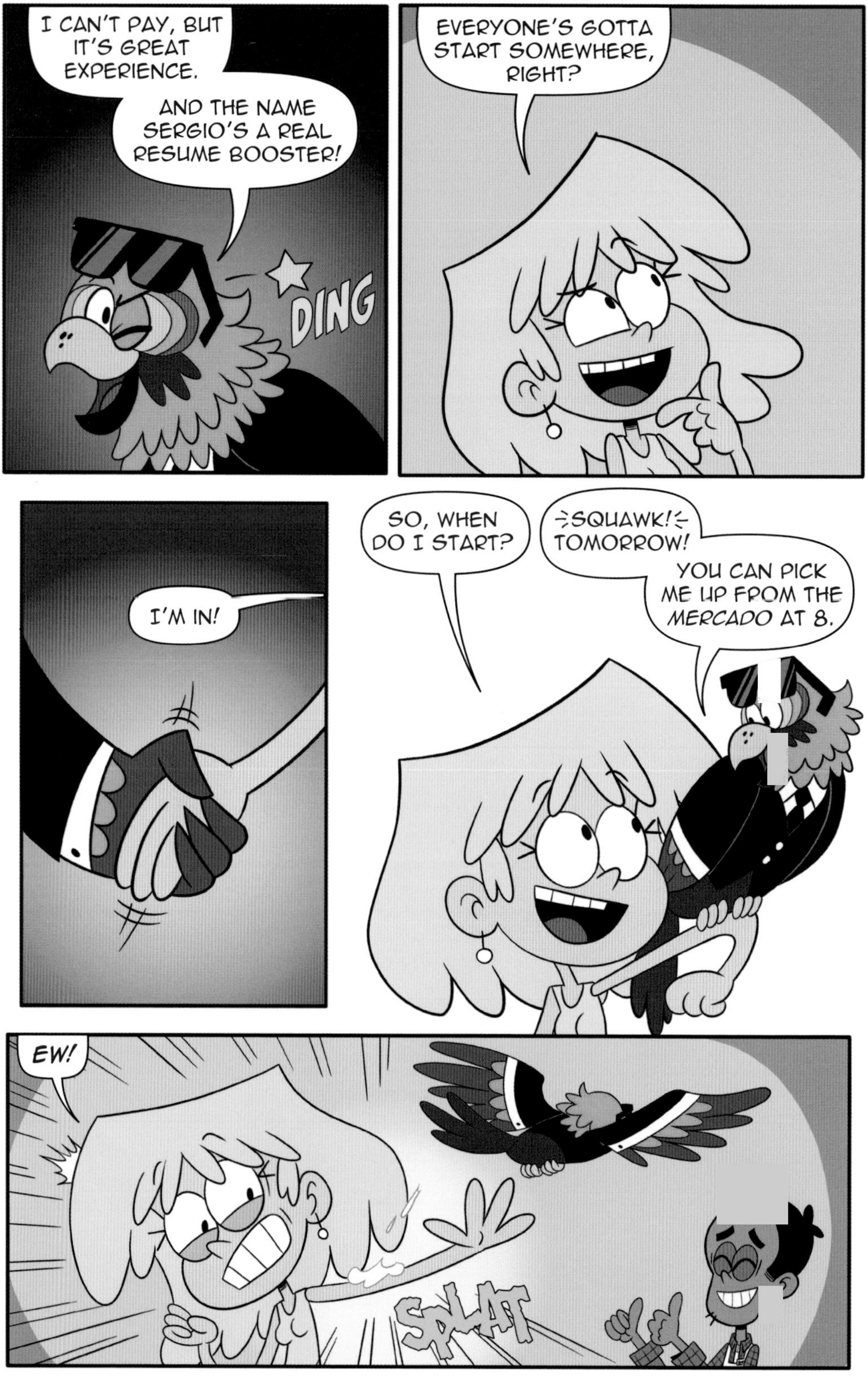
I CAN'T PAY, BUT IT'S GREAT EXPERIENCE.
AND THE NAME SERGIO'S A REAL RESUME BOOSTER!
DING
EVERYONE'S GOTTA START SOMEWHERE, RIGHT?
I'M IN!
SO, WHEN DO I START?
SQUAWK! TOMORROW!
YOU CAN PICK ME UP FROM THE MERCADO AT 8.
EW!
SPLAT

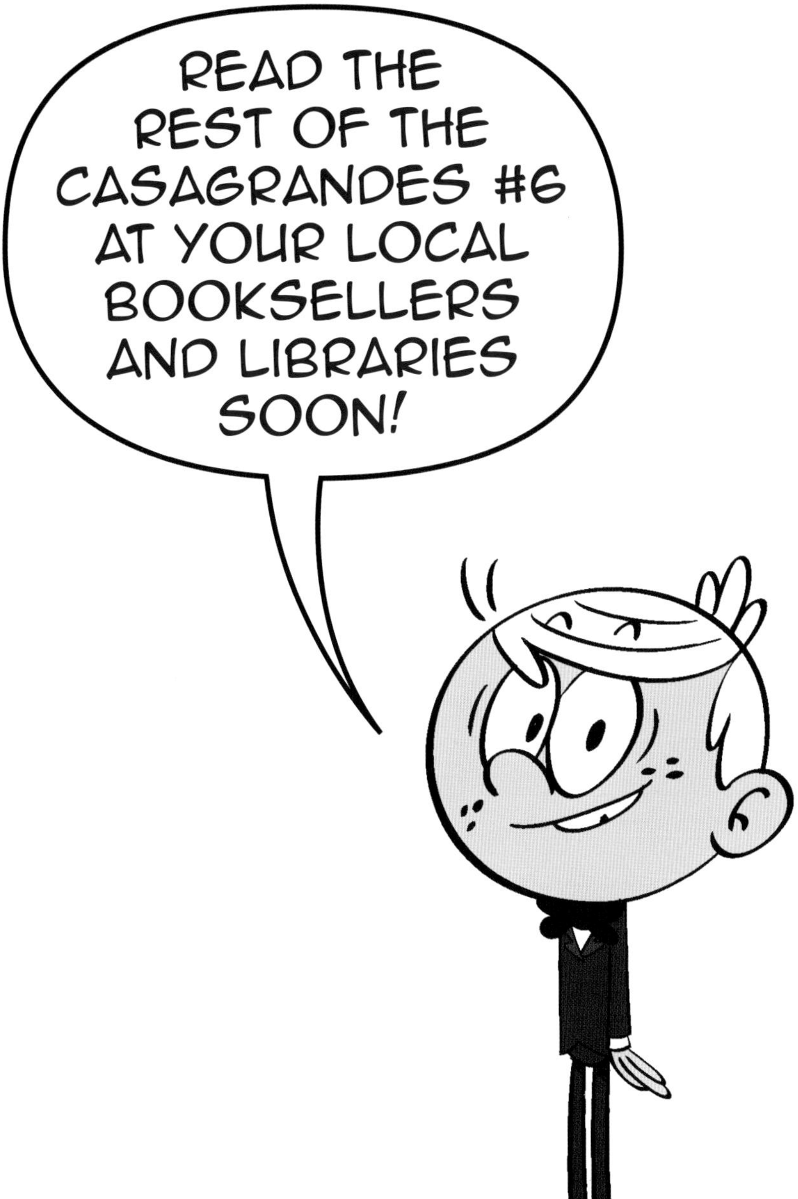
READ THE REST OF THE CASAGRANDES #6 AT YOUR LOCAL BOOKSELLERS AND LIBRARIES SOON!

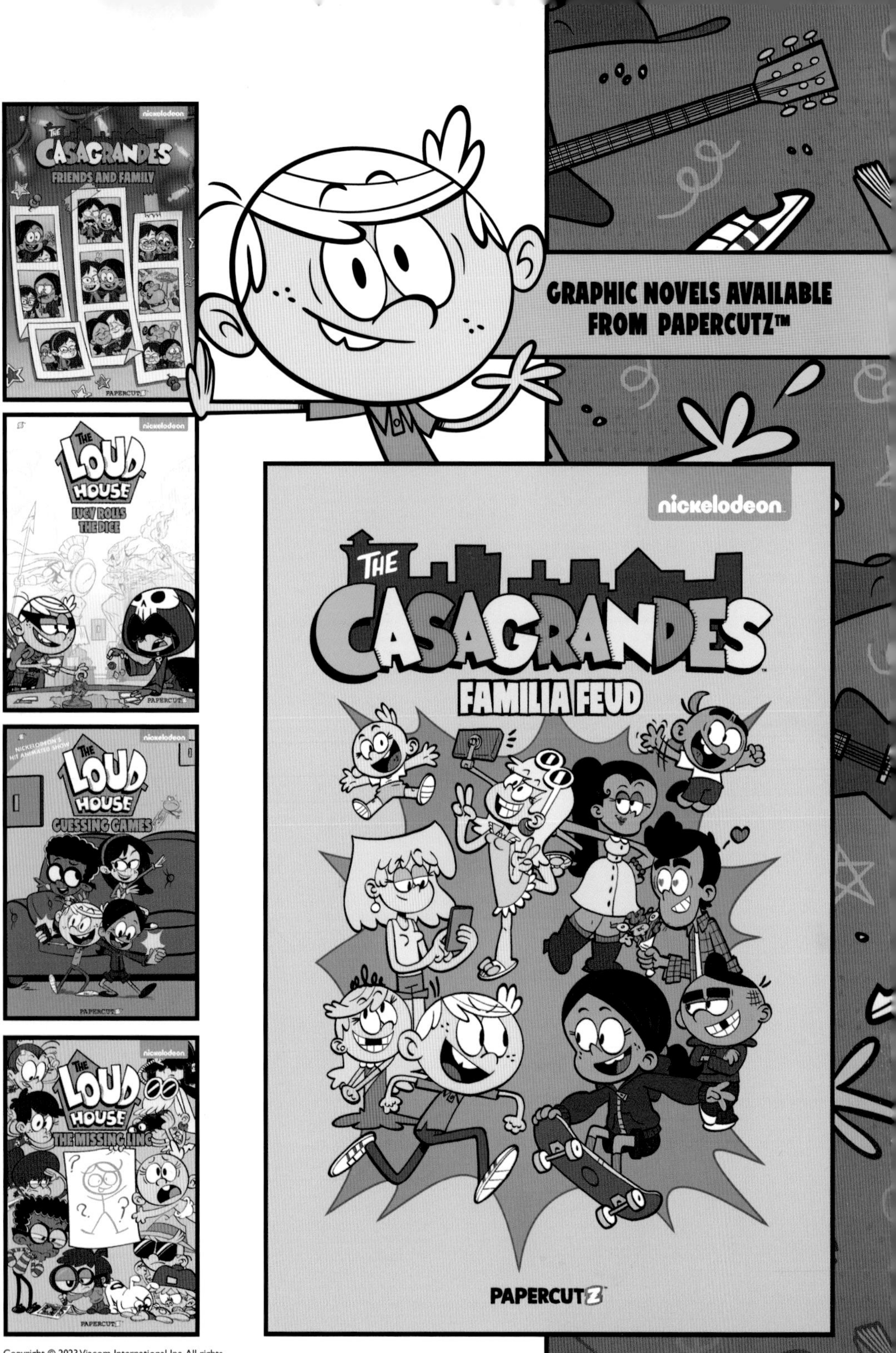
GRAPHIC NOVELS AVAILABLE FROM PAPERCUTZ™
nickelodeon
THE CASAGRANDES
FRIENDS AND FAMILY
PAPERCUTZ
nickelodeon
THE LOUD HOUSE
LUCY ROLLS THE DICE
PAPERCUTZ
NICKELODEON'S HIT ANIMATED SHOW
nickelodeon
THE LOUD HOUSE
GUESSING GAMES
PAPERCUTZ
nickelodeon
THE LOUD HOUSE
THE MISSING LINC
PAPERCUTZ
nickelodeon
THE CASAGRANDES
FAMILIA FEUD
PAPERCUTZ

PAPERCUTZ

@papercutzgn / papercutz.com